Copyright © 2019 Anne Mason
All rights reserved
ISBN-13: 9781071423554

1

The door to the cottage opened and a young man stepped out. As Edmund came into the doorway the morning sun highlighted the perspiration on his face making it shiny; his stomach wobbled and he grunted with the effort of lifting his leg across the door-sill. He looked down the yard to where the furnace stood, around which a group of men were drinking tea. The sound of cheerful banter reached his ears and he frowned. *Pa has been dead less than a week and these men are laughing – and they are being paid to work!* He strode down the yard with as much dignity as he could but being only five feet three inches tall and very fat made it difficult. As he approached some of the men looked at each other and one or two smiled.

'You've been supping tea for long enough,' he barked. There was a muttering and a man, who had had his back to Edmund, turned to face him; all the other men looked, their eyes darting between them.

'Most of us have been at a blocked drainage channel beyond Southtown since long before sunrise. It was cold work and we've barely started our tea,' the man said.

'I don't care,' Edmund growled, 'I know you were my father's favourite, Henry, but it doesn't give you the right to make the rules. You're here to work.'

'But it was your father who made this rule. In fact, if I remember, he suggested it – said that when we came in cold we should all start with a cup of tea and a warm by Bessie.' The two men looked hard at each other for a long time and then, without another word, Edmund turned around and walked back to the cottage. One of the younger men stood up and wobbled himself in mimic of Edmund until he caught Henry's eye and very quickly sat back down again.

'Finish your drinks and then get to work promptly,' said Henry as he looked about the group. The men nodded.

When the yard had re-opened after Robert's funeral, Edmund had left the cottage door open as his father had done. He had wandered about giving orders and tried to deal with things as he had seen his father do but often he found he didn't know what to say when the men asked him questions. Each evening, after the men had gone, Edmund asked Henry and was able to answer the men the following day as if he'd worked it out for himself. However, the men knew of Edmund's ineptitude. Unaware that the men were not fooled, he was quite pleased with how he was running the yard and was happy. Then, one day three weeks after the funeral, he came to Henry as the last of the men were leaving. Henry was picking up his jacket. Edmund went to speak but Henry held up his hand.

'I'm going home. In fact, I'm not going to stop at the end of the day any more – I'll be going at the same time as the other men.'

'But you always spoke with Pa at the end of the day!' Edmund exclaimed.

'Yes, we discussed the running of the yard and sometimes I had ideas that your father had not thought of – but these questions that you ask me he would never have done,' replied Henry. 'I've been helping you these last few weeks but I'm finding it tiresome. Yes, I stayed behind with your father – but not because he didn't know what he was doing – I stayed because he valued my opinion.'

'But the men ask me, and I do not know so I need to ask you,' bleated Edmund.

'You've been adamant for years that, after your father's death, the yard would be yours, not mine – but you do not know how to run it or you would not need to come to me every time one of the men asks you something. If it hadn't been my grandfather's yard, and so means a lot to me, I would leave and take my skills elsewhere – as some of the men are thinking of doing.' Henry looked serious as he spoke and he stared into Edmund's face as he tried to work out what impact his words were having. There was no reply so Henry turned, left the yard and went home.

The following afternoon Mr Stokes, from a mill by Caister, called at the yard.

'My sails need replacing. Can Spandlers do the work?' Edmund hesitated.

'Of course we can,' called out one of the men and Edmund nodded.

'If I come back next week will you have a price ready?' Edmund nodded again. As Mr Stokes turned and left Edmund's eyes stared after him as his mind whirled. He had never understood sails and was unsure how he would work out a price. Then he turned to his cousin.

'Henry, I value your opinion now. Can we do this work? If you think we can, leave what you're doing now and go into the office and work out a price for Mr Stokes.' For a moment Henry looked as if he was going to refuse but then he got up from the bench where he was sitting and went into the cottage.

At the end of the working day Edmund was standing a couple of paces away from the cottage watching the men as they turned down the passage from the yard to the door leading into North Road. He remembered his father doing this some days and, when he did, the men left with a smile and a 'good-day, Mr Spandler, Sir,' but today they smiled at each other or just ignored him as if he wasn't there. The last of them had left and he was just about to turn and go back into the cottage when Henry appeared next to him.

'I've left the figures on the desk in the office. Your Ma will need to sign them,' said Henry. Edmund scowled.

'I'm the master-in-charge around here,' he declared.

'Yes, you are,' replied Henry, 'but you know that your father made it a condition that you would show work to your mother to sign – and besides, you asked me to work out a price because you were incapable of doing it yourself. So, however much you shout about being the master-in-charge, you still have to show it to your mother.' Edmund stared at his cousin for a few moments and then, turning as quickly as his quivering body would allow, went into the cottage. Henry shrugged and left the yard.

I'm going home now, to my Mary-Ann and the children. I have to remember that they are the focus of my life now, not the yard. Yes, I'll keep it going because it was Grandfather's yard and I promised him – and I need to support my family, it is my place of work. I will make sure the yard is successful – because I need the money for my girls to be attractive to a wealthy man and so raise the status of my family – and I'll do it in spite of Edmund. He smiled to himself as he imagined his family at home: they gave him a happiness that offset the frustration that his cousin caused.

'I'm not staying here!' Edmund muttered loud enough for his mother to hear as he went to answer the door to the cottage for the third time the following morning. He had an inkling that the men were knocking deliberately, because now he had shut the door and hidden himself away, and in that he was probably right. His mother, dressed in black, looked at his back as he went to the door. Her eyes were sad and her lips were pressed tightly together.

Henry had been out to a faulty pump at Reedham: it wasn't a difficult job and he could get there and back easily on the train, which he enjoyed. When he arrived back at the yard that afternoon Mary, Edmund's mother, was standing by the cottage door.

'He left this morning,' she told him, 'I heard the front door and when I reached it and looked out he was just going down the passage with a large bag on his shoulder.'

'Did he say where he was going?'

'He said nothing, not even goodbye,' she paused, 'he was not happy with me last night when I refused to sign the work he showed me.'

Henry frowned, 'But why?'

'I wouldn't sign it because he'd altered it. He said you'd done it far too cheaply and he wanted the yard to make a profit now that he had taken over. He had doubled all the figures.'

Henry stared in amazement. 'Doubled!'

Mary nodded. 'When I said I wouldn't sign it he tried everything – shouting, banging the table – he even started to cry in the end like he used to do when he was little and I'd said no to something!'

'I won't tell the men just yet,' Henry said as he turned to start the day's work.

It is good that Mary seems to have a new strength – I'd wager Ed doesn't like it – I hope he's gone down to the docks and taken the next passage to America, but he's probably staying at the ale house.'

Life settled down at the yard. Henry had been right because Edmund now lived at the 'Anchor & Hope', an inn in which his maternal grandfather had bought him a considerable share. He was rarely seen. Henry became happier as the men at the yard quickly grew accustomed to his leadership: more than one of them told him that they were pleased that he was in charge and not Edmund although every time it happened it exacerbated his resentment towards his father and the position he had left him in. If he had not sold his share of the yard and lost the money in London trying to become a rich man, Henry would now be the master-in-charge and not just doing the job for Edmund. He missed his uncle. In the last few years Robert had treated him as an equal and, although they had discussed the difficulties of each job, the decisions were Robert's. Now Henry talked it through with Freddie but the responsibility was his. He was careful to write everything down and bring them to Mary to sign: at first he tried explaining for her to understand but she laughed and said that he could do what he wanted because she didn't know anything about it, but he still brought his pieces of paper and she put her name on them.

He was wary of Edmund.

2

May had arrived and summer was trying to claim its place. This was not the only reason for the air of lightness in Yarmouth; people smiled a great deal and there was an excitement that touched the whole town. In March Branford's boatyard had launched 'Frederica' and the event was celebrated. Now Rust's yard, known as Rusties, had announced that the new brig was finished. Given fair weather it would be launched on Wednesday the nineteenth, in the afternoon, and everyone was looking forward to it.

'C'mon. You not ready yet,' remarked William as he walked up and down. Mary-Ann had taken great care, and many pins, to put up her own hair and was now braiding Eliza's – it was taking a long time. Eliza was trying her best to keep still but she was excited; she grinned at him. Mary-Ann glanced at the two children and smiled: it was good that the hurts of four years ago have been forgotten.

'We do need to be going,' commented Henry, 'or else all the good spots will have gone and we'll not see much.'

'Now patience Henry,' declared Mary-Ann, 'you wouldn't want your wife and youngest daughter going out on a day like today without looking their best, would you?' Henry shook his head and smiled; he was proud of his family and Mary-Ann knew it. However, his remarks about finding a good spot from which to watch had the effect of speeding everyone up. As they left their house in Francis Buildings Harry glanced up the road towards Caister.

'Look there's Uncle Freddie and everybody,' he shouted.

They waited a few minutes for them to catch up. Hannah ran to Eliza's side and the two girls walked along holding hands. Mary-Ann looked admiringly at Ruth's pram: Elizabeth was inside and on top was a new seat where Emily sat which George, Freddie's brother, and his wife Jemima, had sent from London. She looked more closely and saw that the seat even had leather straps so that Emily could not fall off.

They walked to Southtown where Rust's yard had its launching ramp. Eliza and Hannah would have struggled to keep up had they not skipped along occasionally. Although Eliza knew it was not ladylike, and never saw her older sister do it, she didn't care. She was so bubbly with the excitement around her, and so happy surrounded by her family, that she felt almost light enough to join the seagulls in the sky.

As they walked down George Street she became less exuberant: the street was narrow and the buildings seemed to reach down to her. She could see into the Rows – dark little alleys, too thin for the sunlight to reach the ground. People lived in them, she reminded herself with a shudder, instinctively walking closer to her parents. Without speaking she conveyed her fears to Hannah who held on to her hand a little tighter. Young though she was, Eliza realised how lucky she was to live outside the walls, even if only because of the smell: true they caught whiffs of it if the wind was blowing from the main drain towards their house or the air was still in midsummer and the sands began to stink, but usually the stiff sea breeze brought its freshness. She was glad when they came out into the openness of Hall Plain. Ahead of her she could see the bridge across the river and the masts of the boats which were jostling for position.

Henry, to Eliza's delight, went away from the bridge, leading them amongst the trees along the side of the river. There was so much to see that Eliza didn't know which way to look: on the river was all the noise and bustle of a busy port with boatmen who shouted to each other in an incomprehensible jumble of sounds; yet the next moment Hannah had nudged her to look at the large houses of the rich merchants that lived along the river and she tried to imagine how it would be to live in one. Then she saw the crowds and the bunting and heard the band – but it was across the river. Suddenly she was agitated because she thought they would miss the launch.

'Pa! We've taken the wrong way. We need to go back to the bridge,' she called but he laughed and shook his head.

'Didn't you know, little sister?' teased Harry, 'Rusties have paid for the ferry to be free all day.'

'We're going on the ferry?' Eliza asked, looking at her father, her eyes shining with excitement. Everyone laughed at her glee and she laughed with them and clapped her hands, only just stopping herself from racing away with the boys who had taken off at a run down to the wharf at the side of the river. By now Emily was walking between Hannah and Eliza and as they approached the wharf Freddie picked her up, taking hold of Hannah's hand at the same time. Ruth manoeuvred the pram onto the ramp.

'Look after your sister,' Henry instructed William as he offered his arm for Mary-Ann to hold onto, 'Uncle Freddie can't hold onto her as well.'

'Yes Pa,' replied William obediently. He held her tightly by her elbow, digging his nails into her skin so that it hurt. She looked sharply at him and he smirked. The planks on the deck blurred as tears filled her eyes.

Why is he hurting me? Memories burst out from the places her brain had buried them and the fear made her momentarily dizzy.

Meanwhile Tom leapt from one group to another in his desire to get them all on the boat as quickly as possible.

In his agitation he bumped into one of the ferrymen who was just preparing to raise the ramp.

'Careful, young sir, yew'll be 'avin' an accident,' he said, with a wink at Henry and Mary-Ann, 'and we want yews all t'enjoy the launch.' Tom raced up the stairs to the top deck. Harry looked questioningly at this father.

'Yes, all of you boys can go up there. Uncle Freddie and I'll find seats for the ladies here.' Eliza sighed with relief as William followed the other boys upstairs and she immediately put the incident out of her mind, determined to enjoy every moment of the crossing. Her father led them to the back of the boat and Hannah and Eliza sat together. Looking downriver Eliza knew that somewhere towards Lowestoft the river opened out into the sea and she remembered the boats with seamen who spoke with those strange sounds: they would sail that way to places like India which she had learnt about at school and she was filled with wonder that people from as far away as that came here to the very river she was crossing.

At the other side the two families reached Rust's yard and found a stretch of wall to sit on. Fishermen's families, looking to make extra money, were gutting and cooking some of their catch over an open fire beside the wall; the smell made Eliza hungry. The sun was strong enough to have heated the stones of the wall and Eliza felt their warmth seeping through her skirt. Ruth lifted Emily onto the wall between Eliza and Hannah and then put Elizabeth on Hannah's knee while she and Mary-Ann bought some of the freshly cooked fish. They all feasted with their fingers and Eliza was struck by the pleasure of doing something so unusual. Afterwards they ran down to the river to wash off the fish oils, taking it in turns so as not to lose their place on the wall. Eliza went with Hannah closely followed by Henry and Freddie. As they shook their hands in the water Freddie splashed Hannah and she giggled: Henry hesitated for a moment before doing the same to Eliza and soon they were all splashing each other. Then suddenly Freddie swung Hannah up onto his shoulders: Henry was amazed at this but Eliza was already lifting her hands up to him and, catching Freddie's eye and laughing, he did the same. Many in the crowd were shocked at this but others smiled. Mary-Ann, watching them, delighted to see Henry having fun. She was happy at the change in Henry over the last eight months since Robert died. Eliza, however, was amazed by the top of her father's head, which she didn't usually see, and which seemed to have lost its hair.

Returned to her place on the wall Eliza watched a group of people who were on the other side of the ramp from them: these people were not sitting on the wall but were round a large table underneath a huge sunshade and were dressed in fine clothes. Henry had seen them as well and he had just turned to say something to Mary-Ann when he turned back to look more closely: he saw the unmistakeable shape of his cousin. Although he knew that Spandlers were important millwrights he wondered how Edmund had managed to get an invitation. Eliza felt sorry for the children in the group because, while she was enjoying sitting with the sunshine on her back, they were sitting still in a group under the shade. Her brothers, were now playing cricket with a piece of driftwood and a ball Pa had made out of the leather from a worn-out pair of boots; some other boys had joined in and Eliza wondered whether the rich boys opposite were envious, and also, not for the first time, wished she was a boy. However, at least she wasn't one of those girls opposite in their long, heavy-looking dresses and large round hats. She was wearing her bonnet of course and, although her skirt was an old one of Caroline's that her mother had repaired and came almost to her ankles, she was sure she was more comfortable than the girls opposite even if they did look rather grand. Just then a commotion broke through her thoughts: everyone around her was standing up.

'Do you want to see, little sister?' asked Harry. He was her eldest brother and, at nearly fourteen, had been working for almost a year. He considered himself a man and was determined to show himself as strong as his father. Eliza nodded, with a grin, and Harry hoisted her up on his shoulder. Although she had seen quite a few ships launched, it still made her gasp: the ship towered above them as it was slowly lowered down the ramp; it creaked; the wood in contact with the ramp squealed loudly and this, together with the nearness of the huge, moving object, made her clench her fists and grin with excitement and fear.

'Nil Desperandum,' read Eliza's father as the bow came level with them, 'that's a good name for a ship.'

'What does it mean?' Mary-Ann asked. Henry looked quizzically at his two eldest sons to see if they knew.

William shrugged his shoulders. 'Something to do with not despairing I suppose,' he replied.

'Har' t'do when the boat's pitchin' in the gale,' said a voice from next to the wall behind them. They looked round to see a young man about the same age as Harry grinning up at them. Eliza smiled until she saw father looking crossly at her. She quickly turned back but not before she noticed Tom give him a quick wink.

As they left the ferry and made their way home pieces of paper were being given out to the men. Eliza was curious but knew better than to ask her father what it was; he would tell her if he considered that she should know but if he did not, he would not. However, she would not have to wait long.

As they walked along Mary-Ann noticed the two girls talking together and looking at their parents hesitatingly.

'What do you two want then?' she asked as they reached Francis buildings.

'Can Eliza come to our house now?' Hannah asked Mary-Ann. The two mothers looked at each other but shook their heads.

'Not tonight because it's school tomorrow and it's been a busy day,' replied Mary-Ann, 'but perhaps on Saturday?' She looked at Ruth questioningly and Ruth nodded. The two girls hugged each other happily.

'I'm pleased to see you're such good friends,' said Ruth and Mary-Ann nodded in agreement.

Eliza and her family returned home to a wonderful smell. Before they left Mary-Ann had put marrow bones and onions on to stew; she now added swede, carrots and potatoes and before long they sat down to huge bowlfuls of soup. As they finished, Henry took the piece of paper from his pocket and laid it on the table. Eliza tried to read it upside down but quickly stopped when Tom nudged her: she looked up to see Henry waiting for her attention.

'Britannia pier, grand opening, July the thirteenth,' he read in the voice of an announcer. Eliza heard the excited notes in his voice and saw the smile. She rubbed her hands together and her eyes shone. Her mind was bursting with imagination: another day out with the family and her father in a happy mood.

'So are we going, then?' Tom asked impatiently.

'It all depends. I'm sure I'll get the day off, but whether Smithsons will let Harry have another holiday, I don't know. And as for you others having a holiday from school…'

'Father, you're teasing,' declared William, giving his father a friendly push. They all laughed and then everybody quietened and looked at Henry in expectation. He resumed reading.

'Members of the public will be invited onto the pier from four o'clock.'

'Perhaps a half day off then,' interrupted Harry.

His father just nodded and continued reading: 'A local holiday has been declared by the Municipal Borough Council and all the schools will be closed that day.' Tom, William and Eliza looked at each other and grinned.

3

Three months later Britannia pier day began with a cooling sea breeze but it wasn't to last long: by eleven o'clock there was nothing but sun and heat. As Eliza put on her new frock, she smiled: it wasn't brand new, having been bought from the used stall on the market, but neither was it an old one of Carrie's that mother had altered. Harry had saved since long before the boat launch at Rusties and the dress was his gift to her. I wonder what Carrie will be wearing, she thought, as her mother laced up her tiny corset. It wasn't big or strong enough to be functional but this didn't stop Eliza, who was actually only seven, feeling like a lady.

'Have I a beautifully small waist, Ma?'

'Don't you be worrying about that just yet. Having your breath squeezed out of you will come soon enough.'

'Will Carrie have a new frock?'

'I shouldn't expect so. She's not been working there long enough to earn enough for a dress. Don't forget Palmer's take for her keep out of her earnings – and maybe they won't let her come, remember,' Mary-Ann explained. At this Eliza pulled a face. Carrie had been away since just after Easter, when Louisa had secured her a position at Palmer's, and Eliza was really looking forward to seeing her properly. The management frowned on family visits so Carrie could only give a quick smile and wave when Eliza went into the store with her mother and Eliza missed her. Hannah wouldn't be there that day because Freddie Ruth and family were taking their family to visit Ruth's parents in Burgh St Peter so she really hoped her big sister would be able to come.

'Goodness, those are huge!' Eliza exclaimed as Mary-Ann put the petticoats on the floor in front of her and held her hand as she stepped over the wall created by the stiff net to the hole in the middle. As her mother pulled them up Eliza counted three layers and clapped her hands with excitement. 'I shall have a full skirt just like you.' Mary-Ann lowered the dress over her upstretched arms.

'Yes, now help me get into mine,' replied Mary-Ann, the smile on her face reflecting Eliza's as she reached up to take her own best dress down from its hook. Mary-Ann's dress had probably previously been worn by one of the high-society ladies up at Norwich although this didn't detract from the wonder in the eyes of mother and daughter as they viewed it: it even had one of the new crinoline cages that meant that Mary-Ann only needed one petticoat. One of the hoops had been broken when she first bought it and the outer fabric had had an ugly hole where the broken end of the hoop had torn it, but this damage meant that it was within Mary-Ann's means. For three days the huge dress had dominated the living room: clamps had held the broken ends of the hoop in place whilst the glue dried and Henry used fine cord wound round and round the join to strengthen it. Mary-Ann had repaired the rip with stitches that were largely hidden in the folds of the dress so that now it looked like new. Eliza's eyes shone with pride as she looked from the dress to her mother.

'Actually I think I'll put it on after we've eaten,' suggested Mary-Ann, 'I don't want to spoil it.' Eliza looked down at her own dress and frowned but Mary smiled. 'I've already done a fish pie so you don't need to help. I can dish up myself and we'll do the clearing up when we get back later on.' She quickly popped on the simple dress that she wore indoors and was just putting on the collar when they heard a commotion from the living room.

'Carrie's here,' exclaimed Eliza, jumping up and running into the living room. The two sisters hugged each other for a few moments, and then Carrie pushed Eliza away and looked her up and down.

'You've grown,' she observed.

'And you really sound like a grown-up now,' laughed Eliza, yet she stood still, watching her big sister's appraisal.

'Nice dress.' Carrie looked questioningly at her father thinking, not for the first time, that Eliza was his favourite. She was surprised when he shook his head.

'Harry bought it for me,' explained Eliza.

Carrie shrugged away her envious thoughts and smiled. 'Must be nice to be the youngest,' she said as she hugged her little sister again. They went off to the bedroom with Eliza talking rapidly.

A short while later they all sat down to fish pie with Mary's beautiful smooth mash on top. For a while no-one spoke, then William broke the silence.

'What's the food like, Carrie?'

'Not bad,' she replied through a mouthful of pie. This earned her a frown from Henry; she swallowed quickly. 'It's not like we get a home. Plenty though, I'm never hungry but it's not that tasty,' she explained with a grateful glance in Mary-Ann's direction, 'and it's always the same. Bread and cheese first thing, then bread and butter later and a fish stew after the shop shuts. This tastes really good.' She smiled again at Mary-Ann who got up and hugged her in return.

'It's really good having you home,' Mary-Ann said, looking around the table from Carrie to the others. 'I wonder what Louisa's doing.' The room went quiet. Just before Rusties' launch, Louisa, who was eighteen, had left Yarmouth with a young mariner when his ship left port. There had been tears that evening and Henry had asked many times if she was sure – but she was gone and they were still waiting for her first letter.

That afternoon Henry and Mary-Ann led the way down Escourt Road towards the sea, the sun on their backs, and were followed by Carrie and Eliza with the boys at the rear. The sun was hot and Eliza was glad of her parasol and, although she could feel sweat running down inside her corset which was rubbing uncomfortably, she was happy. She was not skipping this time, like she did on the way to Rusties earlier in the year, because her new dress made her feel like a lady and she kept up with the others easily because it was so warm that her mother and father were walking more slowly.

They arrived just before four and Eliza was standing next to Mary-Ann as they waited to be allowed onto the pier. She looked around and considered the other women there: it was true that others had finer clothes, but to Eliza none could equal her mother. In fact, with her own new dress, she couldn't quite understand why everyone was not staring at them in amazement. Henry looked upon his wife and his daughters with satisfaction. Carrie was the more beautiful of his two daughters and was more of a woman, being seven years older. Eliza, though plain with hair that spiked out round her bonnet, was pleasing to look at. He could see how the wedding he'd dreamed about could happen: if his daughters could have seen into his mind they would have been amazed at his thoughts.

On the slope leading up to the large, wrought-iron gates were assembled no fewer than six big carriages and along the seafront there was a whole row of less-important ones. Eliza was fascinated by two young boys, about the same age as William and Tom, who scuttled between the carriages with a shovel and a box collecting the horse droppings and constantly looking towards the gates as they worked. Eventually the gates opened, the boys disappeared and the shareholders and other important people left the pier after their dejeuner that had been held to celebrate the opening. When all the grand carriages had left the lesser ones moved onto the slope to collect their passengers and eventually people started to be allowed onto the pier. Eliza looked at her father impatiently but he wasn't starting to move, so she had to wait. Harry looked at her and saw the frustration in her face as the gates were closed again.

'It's alright Eliza, we'll be moving soon,' he explained. 'The stallholders are allowed on first so that they are ready for us all.'

Then at four o'clock precisely the gates were re-opened.

'What's that they're selling over there?' Tom asked, pointing along the pier.

Harry screwed up his eyes as he looked to where Tom was pointing. 'Penny Licks, it says.'

'They're licking something white,' observed Eliza, 'I wonder what it is.'

'Mmm,' Henry looked at Mary-Ann. 'I suppose threepence for the younger three is not too bad. Carrie and Harry will have to buy their own.'

Harry nodded cheerfully and looked at Carrie, 'I'll buy you one.' She beamed in reply.

'Me first,' demanded Eliza as her father walked to the kiosk.

'I put some ice cream on this cone of glass. You lick it off and give me the glass back,' explained the man to Henry as he put a splat of the white stuff on the cone. The customer he was serving, a young girl, took the cone; she had bright shining eyes and flushed cheeks.

'Nice to see 'em so 'appy,' said the woman standing with the young girl, with a smile at Mary-Ann who nodded in agreement. No-one realised that the girl was already feeling peculiar. The man wiped the cone but this did not remove the invisible bacteria from the glass: they were removed by the moisture of Eliza's tongue as she sought to have every last morsel of the delicious ice cream.

It was eight days later that Eliza began to feel unwell.

4

At one point, near the beginning of the fever, Eliza opened her eyes and knew immediately she was very ill because the fire was lit in the bedroom grate. She could hear her mother in the kitchen downstairs but did not have the strength to call out. A few moments later Mary-Ann came in and stood watching, a pair of scissors in her hand: she found Eliza lying face down with her head hanging over the edge of the bed, quiet and still, asleep; her hair, tied with ribbon at the base of her neck, dangled past her shoulders and Mary hacked it off just above the ribbon. She knew that Eliza's hair would only be a burden to her in what was to come.

Twenty-four hours later the scene was very different. Eliza was terrified: her body steamed and burned and her skull felt too small for her head; coughing woke her, hurting so much that she felt as if her insides were being scraped; her arms flailed about and she pushed off the blankets. Her body craved rest: consciousness faded and sleep reclaimed her – but only for a few minutes before her cough reflex forced her awake again.

The doctor was sent by Mr Blythe, the master of the workhouse next door, who knew Henry. He watched Eliza for a few moments and then turned to Mary-Ann and Henry, shaking his head.

'Keep her warm, really warm – so the fever can burn itself out – and no drinks, or just a couple of spoons of water night and morning. It's probably the measles. Three died last week – now they were weak, undersized little things from near the Plough on Rampart Row and she's strong but you must prepare yourselves for the worst.' No-one realised that Eliza, although appearing to be unaware of her surroundings, had heard all that had been said. Fear arrested her breathing.

'Eliza!' Mary-Ann put one arm underneath her and half lifted her from the bed, shaking her hard so that she took several big gulps of air. Her head fell back on Mary-Ann's arm.

'Eliza,' said her father. His deep, yet calm, voice, aroused her response and her eyes flickered open briefly. Mary-Ann, letting out a sigh, laid her gently back on the bed.

The doctor shook his head again as he reached for his hat and cane. 'I'm sorry. There is nothing I can do,' and with that he left. Eliza lay there: although her eyes were closed she was not asleep.

Die the doctor said. Die and then they'll put me in a box and put the ground on top like they did with Uncle Robert. I won't be able to do anything. I won't see anyone. I'm only a little girl but Uncle Robert was old. No, that's not fair, I haven't had a turn at being a grown-up yet. I'm not going to let them do that to me.

Mary-Ann stayed with her day and night. Each day Ruth cooked enough for both families and each evening Harry or William would go to her with a pot and bring something home. Two days later Clarissa, Mary-Ann's sister-in-law, arrived from the farm. By this time Eliza was still again; her lips were cracked and her breath came in short shallow rasps. Clarissa was horrified when she saw Mary-Ann pour just two spoonsful of water into Eliza's mouth. Eliza moaned.

'She needs more than that. Can't you see she's thirsty? She's so hot.'

'Doctor said that liquid would cool the fever so it couldn't burn itself out,' Mary-Ann explained.

Clarissa snorted. 'Medical men. Just say what they think. Don't really know. For goodness sake give her some more water.'

Mary-Ann hesitated. 'Clarissa, you're not a doctor.'

'No – but I've worked with animals all my life. When the cows have milk fever they do better if they have plenty to drink. And do you know what happened to Gertrude, one of the milk cows, last year?' Mary-Ann looked at her, curiously. 'She had a high fever and Joe, the stable lad, fell with a bucket of water – went all over her. Following day she was as right as rain.'

'What, you think I should throw a bucket of water over her?' Mary-Ann's voice registered her incredulity.

'No, silly. But you could wipe her face with a wet cloth,' Clarissa threw her an exasperated glance, 'and give her some more water will you, or I will.' Mary-Ann propped Eliza up and offered her the cup of water. She drank it all. Her eyelids flickered open: although everything was white and she struggled to focus, she knew that one person there was her mother.

'I'll stay in here with her tonight. You go and get some sleep,' suggested Clarissa. Mary-Ann looked at Eliza, who moaned a little before her eyes closed again. She wondered why she had put her faith in what the doctor had said because she remembered the farm, remembered helping her mother. They'd been so grateful that Mr Blythe had sent the doctor, and she'd been so overawed by him, that she'd just done what she'd been told.

'It's been really hard,' Mary-Ann said and then added in a whisper, with tears in her eyes, 'I thought she was going yesterday afternoon.'

'She'll pull through. You'll see. She's a strong 'un.'

'I know really. It's just that when the doctor told me what to do I thought it must be right. Then when he suggested she might die…,' Mary-Ann faltered, 'I forgot what I knew. Now I remember your husband when he was a small boy, he had a fever and Ma gave him lots to drink.'

The days came and went and Eliza began to be more and more aware of her surroundings. The rash came out and, whilst the cough continued, it did not worsen and, although her eyes became red and inflamed, the fever lessened. Each evening a member of her family spent time sitting with her; some read and others just chatted but she was glad of their company.

Clarissa was proved right because the day came when Mary-Ann found Eliza sitting up in bed. She was very pale and smiled weakly. Mary-Ann stroked her arm. The worst was over.

Weeks went by. Eliza gradually became stronger. Although she still spent many hours in bed, her eyes were not as sore as they'd been and she could amuse herself by reading, even though she often dropped her book and fell asleep. She read as much as she could during this time: Father had subscribed to the library and he brought books for her to look at.

As the summer ebbed, she began to go out: sometimes she went towards town with Mary-Ann or Carrie, if she had time off from the shop, and at others she went towards the sea with one of the boys. Now she was better Hannah or Susan would visit and make her laugh and then, a few weeks after the term had started, she was strong enough to go back to school. She found it tiring at first and Mary-Ann was concerned that she'd returned too early. Then one night towards the end of October, Eliza, having tried to race Tom and William down Caister Road, burst into the house laughing, with colour in her cheeks and Mary-Ann realised she was fully recovered. She shook her head at Eliza's hair, which had escaped from under her bonnet, but she didn't say anything: it was good to have her back to normal.

Later that month Clarissa with her husband Richard, Mary-Ann's brother, moved from the farm into Yarmouth. Richard, and his father and grandfather before him, had worked as the blacksmith's assistant on the farm. The farmer had now bought a new, steam-driven tractor and did not keep many horses so that he no longer needed an assistant for his blacksmith. The cottage, which had been the family home for three generations, belonged to the farmer and consequently they lost their home. Lacon's brewery in Yarmouth were looking for someone to look after their stables and run a small forge and Richard found employment with them. Row 142 belonged to Lacon's and, because of this, the sanitation was better than in most of the rows: the drain in the middle of the row had a covering of slates and the cesspools under the shared privies were emptied regularly so they didn't overflow into the cellars of the houses, as happened in some of the rows. This was where they made their new home. Mary-Ann was sad that she could no longer visit the farm in what had been her home as she grew up, but she was pleased that her brother and family had moved into Yarmouth.

During that winter Eliza tired easily and often couldn't manage her usual chores about the house. She spent her time sewing. There was always plenty to do because old clothes were mended or altered for a new wearer and any new clothes were made at home by hand. She quite enjoyed hemming the bottoms of her brothers' shirts with tiny running stitches, the long line of small stitches giving her a sense of accomplishment.

Now it was late spring and six weeks ago Eliza had turned eight: Mary-Ann was teaching her how to darn.

'Look Eliza. Hold the sock over your mushroom. Pull it tight.' Eliza pulled and the hole she was going to mend got bigger. Her eyes opened wide and Mary-Ann chuckled. 'No, not that tight. Just so that you can have an even surface to sew. Now watch me.' They both had a 'mushroom', a wooden tool shaped like the fungus of the same name with the sock pulled over it. Mary-Ann started with a line of small stitches to one side of the hole.

'Why are you sewing there? That bit of the sock's alright.'

'I know, but you must start from the part that's not worn. Then you can build up stitches into the hole. Watch me.' She made a line of stitches in the opposite direction to the first. Then, on the next line, when Mary-Ann reached the edge of the hole, she made one long stitch before continuing with more small stitches on the other side. Eliza watched carefully: her mother did a fourth line, making a long stitch at the edge of the hole again.

'I don't understand. Those big stitches don't mend the hole. Father could easily put his toe through them.'

'You'll see. Time for you to do your first two rows.' Although Eliza was only eight she was already quite skilled with a needle. She quickly did her first row and then was pulling the thread of the second row through when Mary-Ann stopped her.

'Look at mine. I leave a small loop at the end of the row when I pull the thread through.' Eliza frowned. Her mother explained. 'It's so that, when the thread shrinks in the wash, there's enough slack for it not to pull the mend out of shape.' Eliza nodded, her eyes indicating her understanding. Before long they had both covered the hole with many rows of stitches.

'Now we're going to turn the corner and sew more rows across the lines we have just made.' At the third row, Mary-Ann had once more reached the edge of the hole. 'Now watch me again. Instead of making a large stitch this time I'm weaving my needle up and down under and over all the large stitches we did before. See.' Eliza watched carefully as Mary-Ann started a new row. 'Now on this next row I must make sure to go up where I went down on the last row...'

'...And down where you went up,' interrupted Eliza laughing as she realised what they were doing. 'It's like we're the weaver making a new bit of cloth to cover the hole.' Mary-Ann nodded, smiling at the quickness of her daughter.

Just then the door opened: Carrie stood there with all her bags.

'What...?'

'They've sent me home.' Carrie stepped over the doorframe. 'Can't stop being sick.' Mary-Ann looked up and frowned. Carrie continued, 'It's when I smell food. Turns my stomach.' Carrie sat down and looked at what Eliza was doing.

'Hope you're better at that than I am,' she said to Eliza, speaking quickly, 'mine tend to be a horrible lump in the sock and then Father complains.'

'It's hard but I think I'm getting it,' replied Eliza, frowning with concentration. Carrie laughed – a strange high-pitched laugh. It went quiet for a few moments. Carrie looked at the floor.

'Any of the others at the shop the same?' Mary-Ann asked. Carrie shrugged. 'Why does it have to be you?' Mary-Ann continued, 'I suppose you've lost your job?' Carrie glanced up briefly but at the intensity of her mother's gaze she looked away and started to cry. At this Eliza jumped up, mushroom clattering to the floor. She put her arm round her sister.

'Don't cry. It's not your fault you're sick. It's that horrible food at the shop. Yes, it's their fault – not you.' However Carrie shook her head and turned towards her mother.

'No, it is my fault. I went out on my own. We're not supposed to do that but I just felt I needed to be by myself for a while.' She began to cry again. Mary-Ann stood up.

'Sit down Eliza and finish that sock. Carrie, stop crying and talk to me. Tears won't make it right. Did something happen on your walk?' Carrie nodded.

'A man attacked me.' Eliza eyes widened and Carrie turned red. 'Mother, I think I might be pregnant.' Her voice had risen to a thin squeak. 'You can get sick sometimes when the baby starts growing, can't you? I remember Ruth did.'

Mary-Ann nodded. 'But it might not be that. I'll tell Father you're not well and you've lost your job. I'll be surer in a few days if you really are. Have you had your bleeding?' Carrie shook her head.

'Should have been the end of last week.'

'Oh goodness me – and you're being sick? What about your bosoms?'

'Sore, sort of prickly.'

'Almost certainly you are then.' Carrie's face fell. 'But we'll wait a few weeks before we tell anyone else.' At this point she looked at Eliza who nodded slowly. She continued. 'Sometimes the baby dies inside you in the first few weeks – then you'll start to bleed as usual. No point in anyone else knowing just yet. You just got a bad lot of sickness, that's all. Maybe some water you drank was very stale, do you understand? That's all, just be ordinary. You can start by making us some tea while we finish these socks.' She smiled at Carrie who smiled back in relief and hugged her mother – but Mary-Ann continued in a serious tone, 'if you do carry this baby your life will harder than it needed to be. Certainly you won't marry so well.' This last remark puzzled Eliza.

Why is it harder to marry if you have a baby already? I really don't understand grown-up things.

She picked up the sock again.

Darning's easy though.

5

A few weeks later it was a Sunday and Eliza was in church, sitting in the gallery with her older brother Tom and their cousins Susan, Hannah and Emily. She enjoyed being with her cousins, occasionally receiving a reprimand from the adult in charge for talking and even giggling: none of them liked the idea of growing up and sitting in the pews where they would have to be serious.

An increasing number of people were coming to Yarmouth for leisure. The council, realising that this was bringing wealth into the town, had decided to improve the seafront to make it more attractive to visitors and had built a promenade, called Marine Drive, between the two piers. After the service Mary-Ann, Ruth and Elizabeth the wife of Robert the miller, were talking and Mary-Ann suggested that all the families went for a walk along the promenade that afternoon and met outside the gates of Britannia pier. Elizabeth invited them all to their home in Blakes Buildings for Sunday tea. However, as Freddie and Ruth were going to visit Ruth's parents again, they declined and left in Freddie's new gig. As Eliza watched them go she struggled with sudden feelings of jealousy.

The preacher, the reverend Hills, had spoken about charitable works and looking after the poor. This led to a lively debate on the way home.

'I think he's wrong,' said Mary-Ann with passion in her voice. 'The poor cannot always help themselves'

'Yes – but what about Henry Smithson. He's lost his job but he was always turning up late, or not at all,' said Harry.

'Was he ill?' Carrie asked.

'Only the sort of ill that comes from too much drink,' replied Harry.

'Yes, but then there's Joan's Dad,' suggested Eliza. 'He hurt himself at work and so his master just dismissed him without a reference. Now they've now had to sell most of their things because he can't get a job. Not his fault. Could have been us if Pa had been hurt.' She paused. She was still piqued at the thought of Hannah in the new gig. 'Then we wouldn't have any new things at all,' she added.

'Suppose so,' shrugged Harry, not really hearing Eliza's last comment. However Mary-Ann had noticed and had guessed the reason for it. She didn't say anything, knowing that she was going to take Eliza visiting.

'Wasn't the vicar suggesting that we should help that sort of poor?' asked William.

'Was he?' Mary-Ann asked, but then continued, 'I think he was putting all but the very old or crippled together in the same pot.'

Tom laughed. 'Trust you Ma, to think of it in terms of cooking food.'

'You like looking after us, don't you Ma?' asked Eliza.

'Yes – and talking about cooking, I'm going to leave you all to talk and walk a bit quicker to get home and put the potatoes on.'

'I'll come with you Ma,' said Eliza, skipping to her mother's side as she tried to push away her glumness at her friend's good fortune.

Later, on the way down to the seafront, Henry and Mary-Ann walked behind their children.

'Harry's as tall as a man now,' commented Mary-Ann.

'He is a man. Earning a wage. A bit skinny, but strong,' replied Henry, 'but look, can you see, Carrie's still taller than he is. She is two years older, but at fifteen I would have expected Harry to have caught her up by now.'

'He has almost.'

'She's too tall. Worry about her. A man likes to look down on his wife.' Henry smiled and looked down into Mary-Ann's eyes, 'although I only look down on you because of my height not because I think I'm better than you.'

'But you're unusual. Not like most men.' Suddenly she started laughing. 'Look at Tom balancing on that wall – keeps falling off but pretending he did it on purpose.'

Henry laughed – but then suddenly stopped and frowned. 'Look at Eliza though. She's trying to join him.' At that moment, as if aware of her father's gaze, Eliza turned towards them. She saw her father's face and drew back from the wall.

'I worry about her as well,' he said, 'still too quick to run and jump. Not like a young lady at all. Although it's nice to see her so well after last year.'

'There's time yet,' Mary-Ann said, patting his arm with her free hand, 'she's only eight. She'll grow up. You'll see.' Mary-Ann knew that she must tell Henry about Carrie's pregnancy soon but the afternoon was so pleasant that she pushed it out of her mind.

At this point they came out of the end of Regent Road and onto the sea front where Mary-Ann was surprised by the new promenade, just as if she had not seen it before.

'It's changed so much since we used to come down here when we lived in Maria's lodgings!' she exclaimed.

'That must be nearly twenty years ago. A lot of the town has changed since then.'

A few hours later and everyone was crowded into number seventeen Blakes buildings where Elizabeth and Robert lived. Elizabeth was cutting into a huge loaf of bread.

'That doesn't look like it came from any of the bakers I know. Have you made it yourself?' Mary asked.

'Yes. I have my own bread oven in the yard,' Elizabeth explained as she continued to cut large slices from the loaf. 'It seems silly when Robert is grinding the flour for me to buy it back from the bakers for lots more than he sold it. Robert and his brother built it there because we are the only ones to have our own yard. All his family use it. Have a look inside if you want, the next time you need to go out to use the privy.'

Suddenly Carrie dashed out, holding her hand to her mouth.

Henry frowned, 'Is she still being sick?' Mary-Ann nodded and caught Elizabeth's eye. It was enough for her to guess.

'Would you like some potted shrimps with yours?' she quickly asked Henry, 'or I've cheese – mind it's very strong.'

'Strong enough to bite you back,' laughed Robert Flowers, unaware of his wife's purpose in questioning Henry. It was unsuccessful however because Henry looked from his daughter to his wife as Carrie came back in. Mary-Ann could sense his eyes on her but did not look at him. She knew that they would have a conversation about it before the day was over.

Later Robert asked Henry if he would look at the mechanism in his mill. It was time for them to go. Mary-Ann, with Eliza and Carrie, carried on towards home while Henry and the boys diverted to the mill with Robert. Mary-Ann and the girls were just crossing Church Plain when she realised that Henry had caught up with them.

'Eliza, Harry's got something for you. Wait for the boys and I'll walk on with Ma and Carrie,' he directed as he drew level with them. Carrie and Mary-Ann exchanged glances. They walked in silence for a few minutes. Then Mary-Ann spoke.

'You need to tell your father,' she said gently, 'because he will find out eventually.' Henry looked at Carrie.

'Father,' she said formally but then faltered as she looked at Henry.

'I think I know,' he said, 'you've not just got an upset tummy, have you?' Carrie shook her head.

'I was raped. A man attacked me.'

'What, at the shop?' he questioned.

'No, I broke the rules and went out for a walk.'

'When?'

'A couple of months ago. I didn't say anything. I was too ashamed. Then I started being sick. I think they guessed at Palmer's – that's why they sent me home. I'm sorry father.' Again they walked in silence until they passed by the entrance to Spandler's yard.

'Mr Totsfield was the solicitor who read Uncle Robert's will and he contacted me recently to say that his son was interested in you,' explained Henry, trying, without much success, to keep the disappointment out of his voice. 'If they had been at church this morning I would have introduced you to him. You would have been very well off. Now it won't happen.' Mary-Ann was relieved that Henry was being so calm.

'What will become of me?' asked Carrie in a small voice.

'You and the child will stay with us but you will need to find another job. Something for the next few months at least. You might be lucky and find someone that'll keep your job for you until after the baby's weaned but if not you'll have to find something else then. You're grown up now so you will need to earn for you and your child,' Henry informed her.

'I will look after your baby while you work,' said Mary-Ann.

'Th-Thank-you,' stammered Carrie. 'I thought you'd send me away.'

'We couldn't do that.' Henry paused and looked at Mary. She nodded and he continued, 'you were born two years before we were married.'

'Louisa?' In her amazement Carrie didn't stop to think before she asked. This time it was Mary-Ann's turn to speak.

'I was forced as well. My family sent me away after the birth and a cousin kept my baby. When I met your father I was trying to forget all about her – but he accepted her as his own. We told Louisa just before she left.' Spontaneously Carrie hugged her father.

'Carrie, we're in the street,' he protested but she ignored him.

'Pa, you're wonderful. I hope that eventually I meet someone as good as you.'

'What do you think, Mary-Ann? You're going to be a grandmother!' he exclaimed. Mary-Ann didn't reply but, as they'd now reached their front door, she looked into his eyes and smiled happily. She could see the disappointment the but was thankful that it had happened now. A few years ago Henry would have reacted differently.

'Ma! Carrie!' Eliza's excited voice announced that the others had caught up; Henry unlocked the front door. 'Look what Harry has bought me.' In her hand she held a small brooch made from varnished ears of wheat.

'Robert makes them,' Harry explained. 'He sells them in the mill.'

'That's clever,' said Mary-Ann, 'like an extra way of making money.

'Put the kettle on, Carrie.' The edge to Henry's voice cut across the conversation. 'We need to talk.' Eliza looked from Mary-Ann to Carrie as she reached over to lift the cups down from the shelf; her heart hurt for her big sister but if she could have seen into her father's mind she would have been unhappy for herself as well: he had decided that Eliza must be the bride whom he'd seen in his dream. He was determined that nothing was going to stop her from marrying into a wealthy family.

6

'When you've changed out of your school clothes you can come and help me with the mending,' suggested Mary-Ann to Eliza the following week. Whilst they were sewing, Mary-Ann was telling her about the people that she liked to visit and help: many of them were poor as well old. Although Eliza's family did not have a lot to spare, Mary-Ann would share what she could with them.

'You could come with me if you like, on Saturday.'

Eliza's eyes grew wide. 'What – into the Rows.'

Mary-Ann nodded. 'I think you're old enough now.'

Saturday morning arrived.

'Just put on your ordinary household clothes,' Mary-Ann called to Eliza. 'We don't want to appear well off down there, and it will be very dirty underfoot.'

'But we're not well off!' exclaimed Eliza.

'You'll see,' replied Mary-Ann. A few minutes later she came bustling into the girls' side of the bedroom.

'Come on Eliza, are you not ready yet? Let me help you with that.' Eliza was fumbling with the ribbons on her bonnet; the bow would not come right and it was difficult because even if she stood on tiptoe she could not see in the mirror properly. While Mary-Ann tied it she looked at her and gave a reassuring nod. 'Are you nervous? Going into the Rows for the first time is a big thing, even with me.'

Eliza gave a little giggle. 'Yes I suppose I am – nervous and excited all at once. They look so dark when you peer down them from the market.'

Eliza had been warned against going into the Rows so many times that, now, although she wouldn't have admitted it, she was scared. Her tummy hurt and she felt nauseous – whether it was the thought of going there or the anticipation of the smelliness, she didn't know.

'Well old Joe will be pleased to see us. I told him last time I'd bring you.' Mary-Ann picked up the fish pie that was the leftovers from their meal, put it in her basket and they set off. However as they stepped outside Eliza looked up to see darkened skies.

'Mother I think we're going to have a storm.'

'Yes 'Liza, that's why we're going now – to help Joe with his storm boards.'

'What are they?'

'Stop all the wet and muck from coming into his house when the rains come.' Eliza looked puzzled. 'You'll understand when you see.'

They walked down the Row from the Market Square, and, as they approached the river, the slope became steeper. Eliza followed her mother, walking to one side to avoid the open drain in the middle. She had to look down to make sure where she was putting her feet but tried hard not to recognise the objects she was seeing in the drain. One of the doors was open and she saw a baby asleep just inside the door with its suck-rag in its mouth: the room was dark and she didn't see someone in the back of the room looking at her. They had almost reached the end of the Row when Mary-Ann stopped.

'Here we are, and just in time,' said Mary-Ann as raindrops were starting to fall. Old Joe was waiting for them and had the door open. They entered and before he closed the door Joe emptied his slops bucket into the open drain: it smelt so bad that Eliza thought it had more than kitchen waste in it. Mary-Ann picked up one end of a wooden plank.

'Get the other end Eliza and put it here over the door.' Eliza did that and they did the same with a second plank to make a sort of wall across the door. Joe picked up a stick and began to stuff old rags into any spaces between the planks, the floor and the door. The rags had been used for this purpose before and Eliza shuddered at the smell. She caught her mother's eye and Mary-Ann put a finger to her lips. Eliza was puzzled: they didn't do this to their front door in Francis Buildings just because it had started to rain. She could not work out why Joe needed the planks across his front door and why he was doing that with the smelly old rags.

Joe finished and turned from the door. He looked at Mary-Ann and pointed to his chair. She shook her head.

'It's alright Joe, you sit down.' It was then that Eliza noticed that one of his feet appeared to have no shoe. She looked closer and realised that the foot was made of wood. He saw her looking so that, when he'd sat down, he pulled up his trouser leg. The foot was attached to a wooden pole with a cup on the top. His own leg, which ended just below the knee, sat in the cup and was held in place by straps that she could see disappearing beneath his rolled up trouser.

'Chisel fell on my foot. T'went bad and the doctors said t'was poisoning me so they cut it off.' Eliza's eyes widened. 'Jus' had my stick, but then yer father made me this.' She looked at her mother who nodded.

'It was just a block of wood at the end when your Pa gave it to him,' Mary told her. 'He has carved the foot himself.' Joe grinned with the few teeth he had. Eliza looked round the room and knew that this man was very poor; suddenly she felt very proud of her parents.

Mary-Ann put the tin containing the fish pie leftovers on the fire. When it had heated she put the food onto Joe's plate before putting her pie tin back in her basket.

'Yews not 'avin' none?' Joe asked, 'I 'ave two spoons,' he added, taking them both out of a cracked and dirty pot on the small table next to his chair. He tried to give one to Eliza but she shrank back.

'It's alright Joe, she's had hers and I've had mine. You can eat it all yourself,' explained Mary-Ann.

Joe looked delighted at this news. 'Thanks Maw,' he said and then ignored them while he ate. He didn't eat quickly, as if he was starving as Eliza thought he might, but instead moved each spoonful around in his mouth several times, smiling. At every swallow he voiced his appreciation with an audible sigh. By the time he had finished eating the rain was coming down hard enough for Eliza to hear it on the window. A few minutes later she could also hear the sound of water rushing by and suddenly she realised why he needed the boards. The rain had not only caused the drain in the middle of the alley to overflow but it had turned the alley into a river-bed and water, containing all the filth and rubbish from further up the Row, was rushing past the door. Joe suddenly jumped up and stuffed some more rags around the planks where water was beginning to seep through.

'Thank-yews for comin',' he said. Mary-Ann and Eliza nodded.

'What happens when we're not here?' asked Eliza.

'Mrs Gribbins next door comes in an' helps me. That's if 'er man is in ter look a'ter theirs.'

'But can't she just put the planks across from the other side and then shut the door and go back to her house?'

'Didn't you notice Eliza?' Mary-Ann asked. 'The door opens inwards. They all do in the Rows because the alley is so narrow. If not you might bang someone with your door when you opened it.'

'So what happens then, when she can't help?'

'I jus' push rags in runt'door. Keeps wurst of t'muck out.' Eliza shuddered and thought of that baby she had seen as they'd walked down the Row. She hoped they had their storm-boards up or, if not, that someone had picked the baby up from the floor.'

Later, as they walked back up the Row to the Market Square, Eliza noticed how much cleaner it was since the rain had washed all the muck away. She looked forward to getting back to her own home.

'Trouble with yew, Eliza, is that yer's not one of us. Live outside the walls yew do. Yer think yer's better'n us'. Dorcas stood, a good four inches taller than Eliza, with her hands on her hips. 'I've seen yew, comin' visitin' with that mother of yers. Don't need yer charity, we don't. Look ar'er each other, we do.'

'Right. Yew keep out of the Rows,' added Jane, 'or I'll hev yers.' Eliza stood, her back to the school wall, trying vainly to squash herself into it. Her hands were balled and she felt the roughness with her knuckles as she pushed her fists into the brick. It hurt, but the pain kept her alert and ready to get out of there if there came a gap; it also gave her a focus in which to hide herself from the hate that she felt all around her. Just then Mr Mounseer came out and stood on the school steps, ringing the large handbell that signalled the start of the school day: everyone ran to line up, but not before they had pushed Eliza to the ground. She did not cry; she was numb with shock at what had happened and relieved it was over. But what of the next time? She knew she must make sure that she stayed with her friends.

'What happened to you?' Hannah looked her up and down.

'Dorcas's lot got me. Shouldn't've gone off on my own.'

'You stay with us,' said Susan, putting an arm round Eliza's shoulder. Eliza grinned.

'Was my own fault. You two are good friends.' Eliza looked from one to the other as they took their place in the line and fell silent under the gaze of the master, ignoring the glares from the older girls in the other line.

After school the three of them stayed together near the door that the teachers always used, until they saw Eliza's brothers walking round from the boys' yard, and then they walked home together.

'The older girls have been after our 'Liza again, Ma,' said William as they came in through the door from the street. Mary-Ann was in the back kitchen and glanced up from the bowl of suet dough that she was mixing.

'You just have to ignore them. Pretend they're not there.'

'Hard to do when they surround you and then push you over,' said Eliza with a shrug. 'I suppose they're jealous of where we live really. Told me not to come into the Rows. I'd hate to live there.'

'You're alright with me,' said Mary-Ann with a reassuring smile.

'Yes, until I next go to school. Dorcas saw us visiting when I went with you last Sunday. Told me they don't need our charity.'

'Yes but old Joe does though,' Mary-Ann replied, quietly and firmly. 'None of them care for him because he's really old. Suppose they think he can't do anything in return.'

'But Dorcas said they look after each other!' Eliza's voice expressed a mixture of bewilderment and challenge.

'Like I said, he can't do anything in return, so they don't help him.'

'That figures. Can't see Dorcas Thrimby helping anyone,' added Tom, taking his jacket off and sitting down.'

'I need more water,' Mary-Ann said turning to Tom. 'Can both you and William go so you can take the large bucket?'

'What about Eliza?'

'She'll be helping Carrie with the vegetables. Pa and Harry will be home from the yards soon so we need to start cooking.'

When Henry came in he had some news.

'Mr Olivito from South Quay was collecting some pulleys today,' he said to Carrie.' She looked up from the pile of onions she was chopping; there were tears in her eyes from the onions and Henry felt a sudden urge to protect her. He continued. 'His servant is getting married in August. He wants you to start in the middle of July so that you can learn from her before she leaves.'

'You should have stopped being sick by then.' Mary added. Carrie nodded.

'Thank you for asking for me.' Her voice was muted.

'In November he is taking his family to Italy for five to six months,' Henry explained. 'I've told him that your mother needs help in the winter so he's very pleased to have found someone who doesn't mind not having employment for that time and who can be ready to start when he comes back. We can have the child weaned by then?' He looked at Mary-Ann.

'Yes. It won't be a problem because we've been to see Ruth this morning. She told us that she had another child coming and she's offered to nurse Carrie's baby along with her own so even if they return early it will be alright.' She turned to Carrie. 'You're young. Hopefully he will go away at the beginning of November, so if you wear a corset he won't know.'

Carrie nodded and resumed chopping the onions; the tears started to flow again. Eliza, who had been scrubbing potatoes in a bucket next to her, had listened without saying anything. Their parents moved off into the living room.

'Are you really happy for someone else to look after your baby?' she asked.

'Have to be 'Liza. Could have been in the workhouse. Do you remember Clara my friend from school?' Eliza nodded as Carrie continued, 'well her father told her she couldn't stay in his home because she was expecting a child without a man to support her. She had nowhere else to go. Of course, I would rather have a husband to care for me so that I could look after my baby myself but I'm grateful to be here still.'

'I'll help when I'm not at school. I'm quite excited about there being a baby in our house.'

Carrie smiled at her little sister. 'I suppose that, now it's all sorted out, I am a bit. Still feels strange to think that I'm going to be a mother though. It's going to be hard to be someone's servant because I feel tired all the time, 'she admitted, 'but I'm just going to have to get on with it.'

Eliza looked perplexed but did not reply.

7

It was Monday a few weeks later and it had been William's first day at Smithson's yard as an iron moulder's apprentice. Harry also worked there: Edmund had refused to employ either of the boys at the yard and, although Henry knew that he could have spoken to Aunt Mary and forced Edmund to accept them, he didn't. He was unsure of the future of the yard and wasn't going to insist that they were employed there.

Harry left Smithson's in a hurry, allowing the gate to slam behind him, anxiety causing him to walk briskly; the row sloped uphill away from the river so that when he emerged onto White Horse plain opposite the west gate of St Nicholas' church he was out of breath. He stood still for a few moments, scanning the scene, looking for his brother. Then he spotted Henry leaving Spandler's yard and caught up with him.

'Pa!' Henry took one look at Harry's face and knew there was something wrong. 'It's Will. He's fought with the men. You know how it is on someone's first day – they always have some fun.' Henry frowned. 'When the bell sounded and we put down our tools one of the men grabbed him. The other men crowded round and then Josh – I think he knew him at school – pulled his trousers down. "Let me see what he's got in here," he said. I've a feeling he knew something about Will. The men roared but then suddenly went quiet when they saw. Will wrenched himself free and thumped Josh so of course he fought back. Will seemed to be bigger and stronger than usual, like a madman. Someone pulled them apart and tried to tell Will that it was only fun but he just pushed him over and ran out. I don't know where he is.' Henry drew breath as if he was going to reply but then let it out again without saying anything. They walked along in silence.

Meanwhile a few minutes had passed since William left Francis Buildings, banging the front door behind him. Eliza moved, although the pain in her ribs where William had kicked her made her gasp. Carrie, curled up in the space between the corner and the fire where the pen had been in which they had played as children, was sobbing; she was uninjured but not unhurt. Mary-Ann lay in front of Carrie where his thump had felled her, an ugly red mark spreading across the side of her face from the impact of his fist and blood leaking from a wound in her forehead which had collided with the corner of the fire as she'd dropped. Her skin was pale, her forehead sweaty and she was still. Her eyes, however, were open, staring without focus at the leg of a chair.

Eliza, carefully hiding her own pain, crouched down next to her mother and looked into her eyes. Mary-Ann blinked and let out a sigh as if she'd been holding her breath.

'He's gone Ma,' declared Eliza.

'Carrie?' She tried to lift her head from the floor.

'Shush, lie still, you're hurt. He didn't touch Carrie. Left as soon as you fell.' Eliza omitted to mention the kick she'd received. 'Stay there for a while.'

'I'm cold.' Mary-Ann's voice was hardly more than a whisper and Eliza gritted her teeth as she leant nearer to hear. Her desire to help pushed her beyond her own pain and she went upstairs. She returned with a blanket and was just tucking it in round her mother when Henry and Harry came in. Henry bounded over to his wife as Eliza stood up.

'Go and get Ruth,' he said to Eliza.

She closed her eyes. 'But Pa..'

'Go and get her,' he barked. Eliza turned to go but as she did her body dealt with her pain: she collapsed.

Henry caught her and gently laid her on the floor next to Mary-Ann, pulling out the blanket to cover her.

'It looks as if he's hurt her as well,' suggested Harry. 'I'll go for Ruth and tell Freddie while I'm there.' Henry nodded and Harry left.

By this time Carrie had stopped crying but was still sitting in the corner. She struggled to take in the scene before her.

'Are you hurt?' Henry asked. She shook her head.

'He didn't touch me. He called me a whore and shouted that it was not fair that I was allowed to stay at home while he went to work although he knows it's only for a few weeks until I go to Mr Olivito. He went to hit me. I ducked down and Eliza put herself on top of me. Ma stood between us and he hit her so hard that she fell. Eliza went to help her and then he kicked Eliza.' At that moment Eliza opened her eyes.

'I could make some tea if there is enough water,' suggested Carrie. Henry stroked the face of his youngest daughter.

'I'm sorry I shouted at you,' he said to Eliza as Carrie went through to the kitchen, 'you were trying to help Ma.'

A few moments later Carrie returned. 'I've put on what's there but we'll need more.'

'I'll go to the tap,' said Henry. 'Where's Tom?'

'You've forgotten. He works at the nursery after school now. Won't be back until it's going dark.'

'I'll lock the doors when I go. If Harry gets back before me make sure Will's not with him before you let him in.'

Carrie nodded and her mouth quivered as she lost the battle to stop her tears. 'It's all my fault. If I hadn't gone for a walk from Palmers that evening this wouldn't have happened. And now Ma and Eliza are hurt.'

'No. It's Will. The men pulled down his trousers as part of the fun on his first day. I know he was hurt as a boy but he's going out to work as a man now. He needs to cope with it.' The volume of Henry's voice had increased and now he was shouting.

'Don't hurt him when you find him,' pleaded Mary-Ann, 'let Freddie deal with him.'

Henry looked as if he was about to shout again but then his shoulders slumped.

'I'll fetch the water,' he mumbled.

When Harry had left the house he'd crossed the road, walked quickly out of the town towards Caister for a few minutes and then turned left up Vauxhall Terrace. As usual he was struck by this street with its smart new terraced houses: unlike Francis buildings, which opened directly onto the road, these houses had small front gardens. When he reached Freddie and Ruth's house Freddie was standing by the door, a large earthenware cup in his hand. He smiled when he saw Harry.

'Tea?'

'Is Will here?' Harry asked abruptly. Freddie's smile faded as Harry explained what had happened.

'We need to find him,' said Freddie. Ruth, wondering whom he was talking to, had come to the front door.

Harry nodded. 'Pa's asked for you, Ruth. Ma and Eliza need help.'

'I'll see if Susie next door can look after the girls,' she said as she pushed past them.

By the time they reached Francis buildings Henry had helped Mary-Ann sit in a chair where she was drinking the tea that Carrie had made. The colour was returning to her face. Eliza, however, had fainted again when she tried to get up and Henry was just putting a pillow behind her head.

'We must leave you and go and find Will,' Henry said tersely, glancing at Ruth as he did so, 'but I'm going to lock the doors again. If Will comes here you must not let him in.' Ruth nodded.

'Henry, fetch Clarissa. Row hundred and forty-two.' Mary-Ann's voice was empty. 'Eliza needs her.'

Suddenly the door opened and William fell in. Freddie immediately went to him and led him back out by the arm.

For a few moments no-one spoke.

'I'll go and fetch Clarissa then,' muttered Henry. Harry reached the door before him.

'Stay here with Ma. I'll go.'

As Harry left Ruth came through from the back kitchen with a bowl of water. Gently she cleaned the cut on Mary's forehead whilst Carrie bathed her eye: William was weeks away from his thirteenth birthday and his fist was in proportion to his height: Mary-Ann's eye was already swollen and starting to discolour.

'What about Eliza?' asked Henry.

'I think she's better lying still until Clarissa gets here. She'll know what to do.'

A few hours later Eliza was in bed. Clarissa had bound her chest tightly, which made it difficult to breathe deeply but made her feel more comfortable. She was not asleep. Henry, Mary-Ann, Harry, Carrie and Tom were downstairs. Although it was the end of the second week in June Mary-Ann had felt cold and shivery and so Henry had lit a small fire.

'Shall I read Pa?' Carrie asked. 'We have a new book to start.'

Henry looked at them all. 'Well it would be better than us all sitting here in silence.' Carrie opened the book but before she could begin there was a knock at the door. It was Freddie. He winced as he came in and saw Mary-Ann's bruised and swollen face.

'He's at my house.'

'What? You've left him with Ruth and the children!' exclaimed Henry.

Freddie nodded. 'He's quite calm now. Sad even. That looks sore.' He was looking at Mary-Ann.

'It is but probably not as much as it looks – I think it's Eliza who's really hurt. Clarissa wasn't sure but he may have cracked one of her ribs. She's certainly badly bruised. You say he's sad?' she questioned.

Freddie nodded. 'He wanted to come. He's very sorry. I told him I would see you first.'

'I don't think I want him here. I can't trust him.' Henry put his head in his hands and looked at the floor.

'We've talked about him going away,' Freddie replied. 'That's what he wanted to do at first. I don't really think it will help him if he does.'

'And what if he does it again? He's strong now. Like a man. He could have killed someone.' Henry was shouting. Upstairs Eliza could hear him. She shivered.

'Yes, he could kill someone,' Freddie paused, 'but I don't think he would go that far with any of you. He told me he felt like it but stopped himself. He's upset at what he has done and regrets doing it.'

'I don't want him back,' shouted Henry.

'If he goes away his bitterness will fester.' The edge to Mary-Ann's voice betrayed the closeness of her tears.

'Father,' Harry waited for Henry to look up at him before he continued. 'I will help him tomorrow at work. He needs to face up to it. If we send him away amongst strangers he may not be able to stop himself next time,' he paused, 'and, if he kills someone, he will hang.' Father and son stared into each other's eyes.

Then the silence was broken by a knock at the door.

'I told him to follow me and to knock but stay outside' explained Freddie. 'I can go to him and take him back to my house or …'

'I'll let him in,' said Henry, quietly now. Mary-Ann looked at him, afraid for her son but when he looked at her she nodded and looked at the door. He helped her to her feet and they went to their damaged son together.

When Eliza came downstairs the following morning only Mary-Ann and Carrie were there. It still hurt her to breathe. Carrie helped her from the stair door to one of the chairs. She looked from her sister to her mother.

'He's gone to work with Harry,' explained Mary-Ann. 'He told us last night,' she paused but then continued, 'well, lots of things that he'd never spoken about before. I think he was shocked by what he did and it has brought him to his senses.' Eliza was doubtful. She accepted the cup of tea Carrie handed to her. 'Seeing me like this and when we told him how badly hurt you were – well he cried.' Eliza was shocked. She had not seen any of her brothers cry for a long time. She sat in the chair sipping her tea, her eyes flicking about the room; eventually they rested on her mother.

'So what does that mean? Has Pa decided that Will will stay here as if it never happened?' She began to cry.

'You need to accept it,' Mary-Ann stated. 'He has hurt me as well but your father has believed his promise that nothing like this will ever happen again.' Eliza continued to cry and after a few minutes Mary-Ann looked crossly at her. 'Stop it Eliza. However much you cry it won't change your father's mind.' As she turned from her daughter her lips were puckered and firmly pressed together as if to contain her thoughts.

After a few minutes more Eliza's tears subsided. 'Ma, I don't understand. I'm frightened,' she snuffled.

Mary-Ann patted her daughter's arm. 'You have to see him tonight but then if needs be I'll find out if you can stay with Uncle Freddie and Aunty Ruth for a few weeks.'

'Ma, please don't ever leave me on my own with him again.' Mary-Ann nodded as her own eyes filled with tears.

'I understand how you feel but I think you'll be quite surprised when you see him. This has changed him.' Looking at the blankness of her mother's face, Eliza was unconvinced. She thought about it all day but struggled to take it in.

Later Carrie was in the kitchen cooking tea. Tom had come in from school with a book for Eliza and had left again to work at the nursery. The book was about India and she was sitting in one of the chairs flicking through it, pausing occasionally to look at a picture, but not paying it much attention. She kept glancing towards the door. It was time for the men to come in from work. Mary-Ann sensed her agitation so she leant over to look at a picture of an elephant and stroked her hand to reassure her: at this show of sympathy Eliza's eyes prickled.

I mustn't cry. If I'm crying when Pa comes in he will be cross. Pa – why is he letting him stay? I don't matter; I'm only his daughter. I don't want Will to come near me ever again. But what can I do? I don't think anyone cares about me. I've just got to pretend everything is fine – get on with it, like Carrie said when she was talking about becoming a servant. Yes, that's what I must do.

Her circumstances were imposing upon her the thought patterns of a woman of her time and her family were moulding her will to accept them.

The men entered. Eliza studied her book. William knelt down on the floor in front of her, pulled the book down and looked over the top of it. His mouth smiled but the eyes into which Eliza looked were made from stone.

'I'm sorry little sister,' he said and Eliza's heart calcified at the ease with which he spoke. She was silent. Time paused until Henry spoke.

'Eliza, reply to your brother.' She looked at her father. His voice was hard and he glared at her. She looked down at the floor but still did not speak. Henry took two steps towards her, his arm upraised.

'Henry!' Mary-Ann shrieked. His arm dropped to his side. William smirked. 'Henry,' Mary-Ann repeated, quieter now, 'she's frightened. Look at me.' She pointed to her face, the side of which was now bruised deep purple; her eye was swollen shut.

Abruptly Henry turned towards William. 'Freddie's – I'll take you there for now.' William's eyes opened wide and he looked to be about to answer but Henry turned back to Eliza who was still looking at the floor. He reached his hand under her chin and pulled her face up to look at him; she blinked rapidly. 'Your brother will stay away for a few weeks while you recover but he will be back.' He let go of her and she slowly moved her head until her eyes rested on the sunlight reflecting off the hearth tools by the fire. The mundane became her ammunition against tears: she thought about using the brush to sweep the ash whilst her stomach was a lump in her throat and she fought the urge to vomit.

'That's right, send me away again,' spat William. 'Let her stay. And her!' He jerked his thumb at Carrie.

Eliza stared; her mind pushed ash onto the little shovel.

Henry swivelled William round so that they were a few inches apart, staring at each other. Icily calm now, he spoke. 'We all know you were hurt – but you were a child then. It happened. You have hurt your mother and your sisters and they are frightened of you which is a shameful thing for any man to do. Yes, you're working as a man now – so control yourself – that's if you are to become any sort of a man at all.'

Eliza emptied the shovel into the ash bucket. The scene in the room was the dream.

William dropped his gaze and slouched over to the door. Henry followed him. The door closed behind them.

The sound of the door closing snapped Eliza out of her trance: she cried. Mary-Ann stood up and tried to move her chair closer. Harry, seeing what she was doing, jumped up and helped her before sitting back down on the bench. For a few moments he looked at his mother and sister before pulling the bench up in front of them. He glanced briefly at Mary-Ann then enclosed Eliza's hands with his own; Mary-Ann put her arm round Eliza, pulling her close.

Harry drew a deep breath. 'Eliza, it wasn't just Pa's decision. In fact he didn't want him to come back. I told him that William needed to stay here.' Her large, troubled eyes were unblinking whilst he told her that if William went away he might kill someone and then he would hang. This puzzled her: curtains hung and old Mrs Johnson's bobbins hung next door but how would William hang? Harry explained, as gently as he could. Eliza was upset: she didn't hate William, didn't want to hurt him, but he frightened her.

'But what about me!'

'I promise you I'll always look after you and try to protect you from Will. It will be difficult but we must try, for Will's sake.' Eliza stiffened.

Will! I said I don't want to hurt him, but I feel like a kite with the string broken, floating. Is this my family? They care for him but do they care for me? Harry says he will look after me but he thinks Will is more important. No, I cannot be sure of them. From now I have to start looking after myself.

Mary-Ann and Harry held her but their embrace did not reach her.

8

July came. William stayed at Freddie's. Mary-Ann recovered quickly although her eye was discoloured for a few weeks. Eliza was sore at first but by the morning of the seventeenth she felt well enough to tell Carrie not to put on her bandages: it still hurt when she inhaled deeply but the weather was warm and she was more comfortable without them. She tried to help Mary-Ann and Carrie clean the kitchen and began scrubbing the floor.

'You're slow Eliza,' Mary-Ann observed, 'and you're not scrubbing properly. You need to heal more to do that. Why not go and sew those patches on Harry's working breeches? I think we'd be quicker without you.' Eliza smiled gratefully: she'd wanted to help but then she hadn't realised how much it would hurt until she'd tried. An hour later they had finished and all three were sitting in the sunshine in the yard, sipping tea. A face appeared over the stone wall that separated their yard from the alley at the back. It was framed by an old bonnet underneath which the hair was pulled back tightly.

'Caroline Spandler?'

'Y-Yes,' stuttered Carrie. She stood up. She had grown another few inches since Henry noticed her height the previous year and since her sickness finished a few weeks ago had put weight back on. The face on the wall registered its surprise, its open mouth showing the presence of only one front tooth. With a smile Eliza realised how her big sister would look to the stranger.

'You must be a strong'un then. Mr Olivito wants you to come tomorrow.' Eliza's heart beat faster as she watched her sister's face colour. 'After ten. He will be out by then and I can begin to teach you.' The mouth paused. 'Speak to me then.'

'I-I don't know. W-What do you want me to say?'

'He won't like it if you stutter.' The face was unsmiling.

'She doesn't usually,' suggested Mary-Ann.

Carrie gave a small laugh but then stopped and looked into the anonymous eyes. 'Ma's right. I don't usually. It's just that you appeared and suddenly I was thinking about leaving and the newness of it all.' She smiled and the face relaxed.

'That's alright then. And it seems that you can talk properly. Mr Olivito is from Italy and he doesn't understand Norfolk very well. Come tomorrow then – but don't bring much because you'll only have a small drawer and a hook on the door.' Carrie nodded but the face had already disappeared. Carrie, flustered, looked around her.

'Sit down and finish your tea,' directed Mary-Ann. Eliza, who was sitting near Carrie, watched her sister sit down.

'It's alright 'Liza. Remember I have every Sunday afternoon off so I'll see you each week. You'll be Ma's main helper now.'

'You were going to take me to the fish market and show me how you get the best price. I'll not be any good at it now.'

'Oh, you know when a fish is a bit stale but can still be fine to eat and it's as easy as that. The traders know they won't get anything for that fish tomorrow so they'll take a really low price especially if others still have fresher fish to sell. All you have to do is look grim and move away. When they see they can't get any more they'll give in. They'll probably try a bit longer with you because you're so small and they'll think you don't know. Just show them that you do.'

Eliza grinned. 'You make it sound so easy.'

That evening Freddie Ruth and the girls, together with William, came to Mary-Ann and Henry's for dinner. It was the first time Eliza had been close to him since the assault and at first she avoided his eyes. However during the meal she realised that when he looked at her she felt no hostility. Resolutely she met his gaze and was surprised to find that his warmth had returned. She wondered what he saw when he looked at her because she knew she didn't trust him. Fixed in her memory was the hatred she'd seen when he'd kicked her. It would take a lot more than one pleasant evening for her to overcome that but at least she could speak to him again. She was pleased that it was from the other side of the table that William smiled at her and spoke to her. She wasn't ready for him to come near her.

Later, when Freddie and his family went home with William, Harry and Henry went up to the Kings Arms for a drink. Harry had started going out with his father after the evening meal so that he could bring him home before he became too melancholic and over-imbibed. Mary-Ann, Carrie and Eliza were sitting on the chairs talking whilst Tom was sitting at the table reading. There had been no work at the nursery that evening. After a few minutes Tom looked up.

'I have to read the next three chapters of this book for school tomorrow so I'm going to take it upstairs and lie on my bed and read.'

'That's good. I suggest that you do all you need to down here so that when you've finished reading you can just go to sleep.'

'Carrie,' said Mary-Ann, breaking the silence after a few moments. They were all sewing, finishing off some underwear for Carrie to take with her. 'When you're there you'll have to try and look after yourself. Take all the rest times you're allowed. If you have a task to do that can be done sitting down don't stand to do it. But don't make too much fuss. We don't want anyone to guess. You're young. You're strong. You should be alright.' There was a slight edge to her voice that belied the assurance that her words suggested. She continued, 'however if at any point you start to bleed you must not hide it but tell them and come home. If you can send a message the boys will come and carry you if they need to. But don't just hope it will stop because probably it won't and it is sometimes very dangerous. Mr Olivito will be cross when he finds that he has been deceived but that's as it will be.' Mary-Ann had finished neatening the bottom of a plain petticoat. She went upstairs and returned with a length of coarse cloth. She took a thin strip from the long side to use as a strap.

'What are you doing now Ma?' Eliza asked.

'Making a bag for Carrie. Don't you remember – her other bags from when she worked at Palmers – we gave them to Aunt Clarissa when she moved.' Eliza nodded and watched Mary-Ann while she folded the cloth, sewed it together into a small bag with a flap and attached the strap.

'Thank-you Ma,' said Carrie as she stuffed her underwear into it. She did not need to pack other clothes because she would be provided with a uniform, paid for by her employer by withholding her wages for the first few weeks.

'I should have your corset made in the next few weeks,' Mary-Ann continued. 'You're strong and tall so the baby won't show before then. I'll make it so that it laces down the front and you can put it on yourself.'

'That other servant will have left by then so no-one will know. I'm still being a bit sick though sometimes.'

'That will just be nerves because you're new. D'you understand?' Carrie nodded.

Eliza frowned.

I don't know why Carrie's baby has to be secret. It wasn't her fault. It was that horrible man who attacked her. But it seems that that's how it is because Carrie wants to keep it secret as well. Maybe when I get a bit older I will understand.

That night when they went to bed Eliza and Carrie held each other tightly and they talked. Carrie tried to explain how being pregnant and not having a man was a shameful thing but Eliza was still puzzled. They talked for a long time about lots of things; then, still cuddled closely, they eventually fell to sleep.

The week after Carrie left, Eliza went back to school and she was glad because she missed her big sister and it was good to see her friends. It was the last week before the long holidays when they all had tests. Then, later that week, Tom came home one evening from the nursery with some news. 'They've said I can work full-time in the holidays. You can come as well if you want Eliza. They won't pay you but I'll work quicker with you to help and they'll pay me more.'

'What do you think Ma?'

'How does it feel when you lift things?'

'It's stopped hurting now but sometimes I think I'm still a bit weak.'

'This might be what you need to make you strong again,' laughed Tom. 'Oh, say you'll come Eliza. We can have some fun together while we work.' Eliza grinned.

'But Ma, what about helping you?'

'I think one or two days a week you can stay here, on shopping and washing days, but then when you've finished you can go and help Tom. You'll be tired though.' Eliza nodded but smiled happily.

'It'll be good being outside all the time. And Pa keeps saying Will is coming back. This way I won't be here.'

During that summer some of Eliza's sparkle returned. She enjoyed working with Tom who made her laugh although she became worried sometimes because he didn't always do things as he'd been told and he made Mr Greensome, the nursery-man, cross. She grew strong and tanned although that didn't please her father. Henry kept reminding her that she was a girl and would not be able to do things that made her skin brown and ugly in the future. Henry had always hoped that, with his position as a respected millwright and having educated his girls, he would be able to make good marriages for them and he felt let down by Louisa and Carrie. He was determined to make something of Eliza and hoped that she would grow into a beautiful woman. So far she had grown a little taller but was unattractively thin. Next year he would insist she changed.

Unaware of her father's plans Eliza enjoyed the freedom that the nursery gave her. There were one or two other girls there helping their brothers but they kept themselves in the shade, scurrying out to pick up weeds when the boys had made a pile whereas Eliza worked alongside the boys, doing whatever they did, laughing at their jokes.

The nursery included radishes in their produce: these pungent roots were enjoyed with meat that was often quite strong or salty in the time before refrigeration. Eliza was given some to sell on a tray which went round her neck on a string and was told that she could keep the money from half of her sales. She was thrilled because she would actually be earning some money herself rather than just helping Tom. To the amusement of Mr Greensome she negotiated an advance of a penny on her earnings and with it bought some salt; at home each evening she made small twists of newspaper in which she placed some of the salt. Each day she arrived at the nursery early and made up the radishes into bunches of six, cutting off the leaves with enough stalk left on for the customer to hold; she left the thin root on, knowing that it would keep them fresher. Then she brushed each bunch along the bristles of the yard brush to remove the worst of the soil before putting them on her tray. Around her neck she wore two separate money bags so that she could keep her takings from selling the salt separate from the rest. Mr Greensome chuckled when he saw her and said that she ran a sharp business. She arrived each morning amongst fresh shrimp sellers on Marine Drive and by the time the large clock on the front said half past one she had usually sold out. Each evening she brought home her money and gave it to Mary-Ann who kept it in a pot, declaring that it would be used for Eliza's schoolbooks next term. Henry pondered as to why he had a daughter had all the qualities that he could wish for in a son: she will become a woman and would not need those abilities.

Tom was collecting his wages from Mr Greensome on the last Saturday in August. 'We can only work another week for you,' he said, 'because school starts again the week after.'

'Why young Tom, would yer not prefer t'finish lifting the taters than listen ter the schoolmaster?'

Tom nodded ruefully. 'Pa will want us to go to school. I know he'll say no if I ask but if you come,' Tom paused and shrugged his shoulders, 'well it'll probably not be any different but come and ask him for us. Please?' Mr Greensome agreed and walked home with the two children that afternoon. They listened to Henry explaining how important a good education was to both of them and Tom was downcast. Eliza, however, was quite relieved: much as she had enjoyed being at the nursery and selling the radishes she was also quite looking forward to returning to school. She enjoyed learning and appreciated her books.

William returned home that week. He seemed to be making a special effort to be pleasant with Eliza but she was cautious and hardened herself to his smiles and kind words. She did not trust him.

9

The door to the house in Francis buildings opened with a bang.

'Mary-Ann! Mary-Ann!' Henry was grinning.

'Whatever is it?' Mary-Ann looked round the door from the kitchen; Eliza and Tom, who were sitting at the table doing schoolwork, stared: Pa didn't usually act like this when he came home from work.

Henry chuckled and rubbed his hands together, his eyes laughing. 'A gathering of the family – Aunt Mary – at the yard – she wants us to write to everybody. My sisters may come!'

'What? What do you mean?' Mary-Ann's face beamed at his excitement. 'Slow down Henry. In fact sit down and stop talking. I'll make more tea and by then you'll be able to tell us so that we can understand.'

Henry flopped into his chair and Eliza skipped over and hugged him, giggling at her father's happiness. Tom hesitated for a few moments until Henry looked over in his direction, then moved near to his father's side. Henry put an arm round his shoulders and drew him closer, pulling him off-balance; Tom's forehead wrinkled in bewilderment.

'My sisters may come,' Henry whispered into Tom's ear but he didn't even know that his father had sisters. Just then Harry came in, closely followed by William. They both stopped and gawped at the sight of their father cuddling Tom and Eliza.

'What did you whisper to Tom?' Eliza asked, so Henry turned and reiterated his statement to her. She grinned.

'You mean your sisters, like I'm Tom's sister?'

'Yes, my sisters are Mary and Rachel: I'm two years older than Mary just like Tom is two years older than you, but Rachel is eleven years younger than me - like Louisa and you. Let me think, Rachel left the year that you were born Eliza, that's 1851.' He turned to Harry. 'You're fifteen, aren't you? That means you were seven so perhaps you remember her?'

Harry frowned. 'Did she live with the really old lady who lives near Aunt Mary?'

'Aunt Hannah? Yes, she did.'

Mary-Ann appeared, speaking as she came through the door from the kitchen with a tray full of cups of tea, 'Sit down boys, tek a cup. I think your father has some news.' She placed the tray on the table and everyone reached forward and took one. Silence. They all looked at Henry.

'Aunt Hannah – the one you were talking about just now, Harry – is sixty next month and my aunts, well, they've decided to see how many of the family they can get together to celebrate. But I think it was Aunt Mary's idea.'

'You mean the lady who was married to Uncle Robert who died?' Eliza asked.

'That's right. She's just come and told me at the yard. Since Uncle Robert died the aunts, Uncle Robert's sisters, Hannah – she's the one who's sixty – and their oldest brother William's widow, Susanna,' Henry counted them off on his fingers, 'they've been visiting her each Thursday. Mary told them her idea – they will have talked about it a lot and now it's going to happen.'

'So who's coming?'

'Well Aunt Mary is writing to all her children, that's my cousins. Then she's writing to her sister Elizabeth's widower William. I'm looking forward to seeing him as well. Used to work at the yard before Aunt Elizabeth died. And his children, my other cousins,' he laughed and rubbed his hands together, 'they used to swing on my arms when they were little. That was before my father…' He stopped and, for a second, his smile vanished. No-one but Mary-Ann noticed.

'What about Aunt Hannah and Aunt Susanna what you just said?' asked Tom.

'Whom I spoke about you mean?' Tom nodded as Henry continued, 'Aunt Hannah has no children – I think that's why they're having the celebration – and Aunt Susanna's daughter still lives with her. I'm to write to Rachel and Mary in Yorkshire and Freddie to his brothers in London. I'll write and tell Tom of course but he won't be able to come from America.'

Harry laughed. 'Sounds like fun but where will they all sleep? Even if we all squeeze up there's only room for a few more here and I'm sure Robert the miller and Freddie are the same at their houses.'

'They've thought of that. It's going to be towards the end of October when the holiday visitors will have gone home and the lodging houses will all be empty – although we can probably fit one of my sisters and family in here?' He looked at Mary-Ann who nodded. 'Find me the letter paper, I'm going to write to Rachel and Mary this very minute. I might see them next month.' His eyes danced with excitement as he drummed on the table causing the tray to clatter to the floor.

Great Yarmouth, since the middle of the eighteenth century, had been a place where the wealthy came on the advice of their doctors who prescribed bathing in the sea, or sometimes even drinking it, as a cure for many ailments. The town had indoor, heated, sea water baths. These were not swimming baths but small pools where those who could afford it would be immersed, privately, with the help of attendants called dippers. Bathing machines, like huts on wheels, stood on the beach, from which the more adventurous plunged into the sea itself. Gradually people came just for leisure and fun. With the coming of the railways and cheap third-class rail travel more and more people came and Yarmouth became a holiday resort. Initially the town's people resented these pleasure-seeking strangers but as the flow of visitors increased everyone realised they could make money from them.

Mrs Todd's and her neighbours' houses on Row Nine had a yard with a communal privy where for many years she'd kept a cow. For a few weeks a year she took it onto common land near the river where it would be impregnated by a large bull tethered there. The resulting calf was a sickly animal because, although whilst on the common the cow could graze, generally its diet was poor. However Mrs Todd was unconcerned because she gave the calf to the bull owner, who produced veal, as payment for the bull's services: she wanted the milk and had, with practice, learnt the minimum standards of nutrition required to maintain its production. She allowed her neighbours to collect the cowpats to dry and use as fuel and they were pleased when there was excess milk that they could buy because it was fresh and did not make them ill. In the summer she let the milk stand for a few hours before carefully skimming off all the cream so that her daughter could take it down to the ice-house near the quay where she turned it into ice-cream which she placed in a bucket in the middle of a barrel filled with ice. This she pulled on wheels along the quay, selling it very profitably to ladies in crinolines and others with leisure and money who walked under the trees and watched the ships. Grand hotels accommodated the rich and lodging houses were built on the sea-front for the less well-off. The very poorest holidaymakers stayed with the townsfolk who lived in as few rooms as possible for the summer in order to let out space. Young boys earned money by attaching homemade carts to the family goat and giving children rides along the beach for a few pennies. Eliza's enterprise selling radishes in the summer of 1859 was one of many which harvested the visitors' money. That summer the town was busier than anyone could remember: the visitors had doubled the population. It was a time of increasing prosperity for the town and Henry's sisters and cousins would find it changed.

Excitement grew over the following weeks as replies came back. When Henry came home each evening they would all want to hear if he had heard about another person who was coming. At first Eliza tried to remember them all whilst he spoke about this or that cousin and their various children but soon she gave up. Each morning at breakfast Henry eyed the rectangular slot that he and his brother Thomas, just before he left for America, had cut in the front door and eventually he was rewarded with the sight of a letter coming through the hole. Letters came infrequently, and Henry opened it slowly and carefully whilst Eliza hopped from one foot to the other. Not a sound could be heard whilst he read so that they all startled when the kettle whistled. Mary-Ann went through to the kitchen and took it off the fire. She returned just after Henry finished the letter; he looked up.

'Mary and her family are coming but Rachel's pregnant and doesn't want to have the journey,' he explained. 'I'm sad not to see Rachel – but Mary is coming.' He grinned and everyone started talking at once. After a few minutes Mary-Ann went back to the kitchen and returned with bread, cheese and a large pot of tea. Eliza saw her and jumped up to get the cups and plates but no-one stopped talking.

Mary-Ann started to cut the bread then, unusually, she raised her voice, 'If you don't all stop talking and eat you're going to be late for work and school.' They glanced at the clock on the cupboard next to the table and quickly started to eat although none of them could stop grinning.

After a moment or two Eliza folded her bread over a piece of cheese. 'I'm going to eat mine as I walk to school.'

Tom copied her. All the schools in the town were still on summer timetables and started at eight. At first Henry frowned but then nodded: he didn't want them to go to school hungry but he knew there were painful penalties for being late.

    Later that morning something happened which dampened their excitement.

10

It was quiet at Francis Buildings. Mary-Ann was working her way through the day's chores and had just begun cleaning the hearth when the door opened. Harry stumbled in, a bloody rag on his hand.

'Finger's gone,' he said quietly, his pale face betraying his shock. 'Caught it in the bucket as it lifted.' He shuddered. 'It pulled it off.' He half-sat, half fell onto the bench, leant against the wall and closed his eyes. Mary-Ann stared at him, and then he started to speak again. 'At first, because my finger was jammed, it caused the bucket to sway. I thought it was going to tip up and could see the molten metal slopping towards me. I ducked out of the way and the bucket splashed a bit but didn't fall on anyone. It was a few moments before I felt anything and then I realised it had taken my finger with it. B-but if all the m-metal had sp-p-plashed…' He was trembling. Mary-Ann, hiding her turmoil, took a strip of cloth from the odds and ends in her sewing box. She tied it round the top of his arm, put a wooden spoon between the cloth and his arm and twisted it so tightly that Harry winced.

'Hold this spoon with your other hand and let me have a look.'

Just at that moment Henry came in. 'William came from Smithson's and told me Harry had been hurt. I've popped my head round the cottage door and told Mary. Freddie's looking after the yard until this afternoon,' he said as he sat on the bench next to his son.

Mary-Ann removed the rag. It was clear that the finger had been ripped out at the knuckle. 'That's lucky,' she said.

'Don't feel lucky,' muttered Harry through gritted teeth.

Mary-Ann turned to Henry, 'Is there any gin in the cupboard?'

'A little,' replied Henry as he tipped the bottle sideways. Mary-Ann nodded towards Harry and Henry removed the stopper and passed the bottle to his son. Harry took a large gulp and coughed.

'Steady, sip it slowly, you want to drink as much as possible without being sick,' Mary-Ann told him calmly before turning back to Henry. 'Cut me some nettle from my pot in the yard and then can you get some more gin? He's going to need it while I put this together.'

'What – you're going to do this yourself?'

'Yes. Helped my mother repair a gash in my father's leg.' She pointed to the hole on Harry's knuckle. 'Look, it's left a flap of skin. Should let it heal without pulling on the other fingers too much. Now bring me the nettle and then go and get that gin.' Henry left as Mary-Ann looked at the wound more closely. She had grown up on a farm where the vet was an expense which was incurred only as a last resort and she'd seen her mother treat wounds in the animals. She'd also learnt from her how some plants could be used medicinally. She grew nettle amongst her other herbs by the back door and if the arthritis in her hands was troubling her she would copy what she'd seen her mother do as a child and run them through the nettles before bed: nettle stings were a small price for the numbness which followed when they wore off. Harry allowed her to brush his hand with the nettles; he hardly noticed the stings. A few minutes later Henry, breathless from running, returned with the gin and put another large tot into a cup; Harry drank it without coughing this time. Mary-Ann opened the earthenware pot that she'd brought through from the shelves in the kitchen. From it she sprinkled lavender flowers into her mortar and ground them into a powder. She found a large needle from her sewing box and used the pincers to hold it in the fire: she did that because her mother used to but had no idea why. At first Harry was breathing quickly and watching her closely but as the alcohol took its effect he closed his eyes and his breathing slowed.

'My arm'stharting to ache,' he said.

'Just let that spoon go loose for now.' Mary-Ann watched the wound fill with blood and start to drip while she threaded the needle.

Harry opened his eyes. 'Whacha doin' wisthat?' he asked. The gin was working.

'I'm going to sew that flap of skin down to cover the hole,' she stated, as if it was a patch on his trousers. Henry stood next to Harry. He took the spoon from him and tightened it again whilst he held the damaged arm with his other hand. Mary-Ann waited for the flow of blood to slow and then she sewed her son's flesh, sprinkling the edge of the wound with the ground lavender between stitches. Harry moaned but made no attempt to pull his arm away. When she'd finished she put some water on the lavender which still remained in the mortar and put a pad of cloth in it to soak. Then she squeezed out as much liquid as she could and placed the pad on top of the wound. She undid the tourniquet from Harry's arm and used the cloth to tie the pad firmly in place. Henry sat down on the bench next to Harry who was both shivering and sweating. Mary-Ann positioned Harry's arm on Henry's shoulder with his forearm resting on his head so that his hand was towards the ceiling.

'It's done,' she said simply and went to the kitchen to put the kettle on the fire. Whilst it was heating she went upstairs and returned with a blanket which she wrapped around her son. In a few minutes the kettle boiled and she made three cups of strong tea. 'We all need something sweet after that,' she said, putting a large spoonful of sugar in each.

'Will they let you work using one hand for a bit?' Henry asked as Mary-Ann sat on the bench with them.

'Yesth. Doing that before. Mr Thmith..Smith..He wanths me back Monday.'

'You'll only miss tomorrow morning,' said Henry, 'Mr Smithson's a good employer. He'll move the men round to give you a job that you can do. He won't let you near the hot metal until you can use both arms.'

'Yes it's just as well it's Friday. Give's you a chance to rest it,' added Mary-Ann as she folded part of an old sheet into a triangle. Five minutes later she inspected the bandage on his arm and could see no fresh blood so she put it into a sling. Henry helped him to move from the bench to one of the chairs and soon Harry was asleep.

An hour later Mary-Ann, who was still feeling rather wobbly, decided that they all needed more than the bread and butter which they usually ate in the middle of the day. She took down the bacon from its hook by the fire in the kitchen and cut off a chunk that was mostly fat with some lean. This she chopped into small pieces and cooked it gently until there was lots of liquid fat in which floated crispy bits of meat. The smell woke Harry. Mary-Ann added eggs to some bread and allowed them to soak in before adding the mixture to the pan and stirring until it was set. They ate from bowls with spoons, which was easy for Harry. Mary-Ann watched with some relief as colour returned to his face. Henry went back to the yard and Harry dozed on and off all afternoon. Eliza and Tom came in from school and their eyes widened at the sight of their brother in their father's chair with a blanket round him. He forced a smile and held up his bandaged hand.

'What happened?' Tom asked.

'Lost a finger. Ma's sewn the hole shut but I'll never be able to point at you with that finger again.'

'Wow!' exclaimed Tom and the admiration in his voice made Harry grin in spite of the pain. Eliza frowned, came over to Harry and gently stroked the bandaged hand.

'Does it hurt?' she asked.

Harry nodded. 'Throbs. In fact it's getting worse.'

Eliza turned to her mother. 'Ma, his hand feels hot?' she questioned. Mary-Ann went to the kitchen and took down another earthenware pot from the shelves and from it put some white flowers in her pestle. She ground them up and covered them with hot water from the kettle. After a few minutes she strained the liquid into a cup and took it through to Harry.

'Here you are, drink this. It won't taste very nice but will make it more comfortable.' She turned to Tom after writing on a scrap of paper. 'Will you go up to the yard and give this to your father? I want him to go to the chemist.' She turned back to Harry. 'It's for something for bedtime because it will feel really sore when you're trying to go to sleep tonight. You need something stronger than I can make with my plants.'

'Can I go with Tom?' Eliza asked but her mother shook her head. 'Father will be pleased to see Tom but he won't welcome you when he's working.' Eliza frowned. 'He's a boy, that's why,' her mother explained but Eliza had realised that: she'd frowned because she didn't like it. She looked at the paper.

'What is it?'

'Laudanum,' replied Mary-Ann, pleased that Eliza had not argued. 'It's a very strong medicine for pain, much stronger than the meadwort tea he's drinking now. It'll make him sleep but we must make sure he doesn't have too much or he won't wake up.' At this Harry sat up with a jolt. Mary-Ann smiled. 'It's alright we'll be careful with how much you have. But you must promise me you won't try and help yourself if I'm asleep in the middle of the night.' Harry nodded as Tom left the house.

When Mary-Ann removed the bandages on Sunday evening she was pleased: the lavender had done its job because, although there was some redness around the stitches, there was no pus. She made a strong lavender infusion. Eliza asked if she could bathe his hand and Mary-Ann agreed: she had long been aware of Eliza's natural empathy and wanted to encourage her. As Eliza worked Henry and Tom told silly stories, which distracted Harry. William said nothing but watched her closely.

'It's ready for the bandage now Ma,' said Eliza.

'I'm going to leave it until bedtime, let it have some air,' replied Mary-Ann.

Harry smiled at Eliza and Mary-Ann. 'Thank you both for looking after me. Not having the bandage on will mean I can get used to seeing my hand without its finger and using my others instead.'

'You must be careful not to knock it, Harry,' warned Mary-Ann. He nodded.

'Not a bad little nursemaid, our Eliza,' intoned William from the corner. He made Eliza shudder but no-one noticed.

11

It was the beginning of the week before the party. Henry came home and said that on the following day, Wednesday, he was going with Mary, uncle Robert's widow who still lived in the cottage at the yard, to meet her son Richard who was arriving on a ship from London. This ship, 'Albatross', was one of several which moved goods between London, Yarmouth and Hull: these ships no longer relied on sail and the force of wind to move through the sea because they had the power of steam. This gave them a force of their own with which to come against the forces of nature when the wind and waves would take them on a path that they didn't want to travel.

The next day dawned dark and wet. By the evening the wind was wild and churned the sea. The whole family decided to go with Henry and Aunt Mary, and she was glad of the company of Mary-Ann.

'I don't like this wind,' she commented as she pulled up the hood of her cape over her bonnet.

'Don't worry,' replied Mary-Ann. 'I'm sure he'll be safe. Remember the Reverend Hills prayed for him by name on Sunday.'

'Mmm,' she sounded unconvinced, 'I still don't want to think of him on the sea in a storm.'

When they reached the jetty they met up with Freddie and Ruth, who had left their young girls with a neighbour. They all smiled at each other although the weather had diluted their excitement with anxiety.

'Look at the waves crashing into the pier,' shouted William above the weather's dissonance. The two Marys looked at each other; Henry saw the look.

'Remember he's in a steam-ship so not at the mercy of the wind.'

'No, we weren't,' said a voice behind them. They spun round to see Richard walking towards them. He went straight to his mother and hugged her; she cried. 'The wind was behind us part of the way so we made good time. I knew you were coming so I waited in the hotel foyer. I'll just get my bags.' He turned back into the Bath Hotel, reappearing a few moments later with two large portmanteaux.

'I'll help,' offered Harry.

'You be careful of that hand. Lift nothing heavy with it.'

'Yes Ma,' replied Harry, grinning as he held up his hand towards Richard. 'I'll explain at home. It's hard work shouting above this wind.'

'Come back to the yard for a bit,' suggested Mary, 'then we can talk properly.

'Look at that boat,' shouted William. A schooner, still with most of its sail unfurled, had been caught in the current which pulled across the end of Wellington Pier and was being driven side-on across the sea.

'It's blowing towards the pier,' shouted Henry. A hooter sounded and men raced towards the new lifeboat station as, with a crash that could be heard above the waves and wind, the boat hit the pier.

Eliza stood still, watching. She could see people holding onto the sides as the waves receded and pulled the boat away before flinging it into the pier again with yet more force.

'God, save those people,' she cried but the wind snatched her prayer.

'The pier's collapsing,' shouted Harry as, beyond the boat, the squares and rectangles that were part of the pier's structure became rhombuses and parallelograms; it swayed and cracked before sliding into the sea. By now the family were joined by onlookers from the hotel and other lodging houses on the front. Eliza watched a group of men just below them on the walkway, which ran from Marine Drive under the pier, where there was a tavern, and up the other side back onto the promenade. They were fiddling with something on the ground; she couldn't see clearly but thought she saw one of them light a taper. Then suddenly Harry grabbed her.

'This is going to be loud,' he shouted as he put his hands either side of her bonnet. There was a bright flash and a crack and, in spite of Harry's warning, she jumped and clung onto him. He moved his hands from her ears.

'It was a gun. It's fired a rope out to the ship,' he explained. Eliza could just see the rope but it looked so thin that she couldn't understand how it was going to help the people on the boat. Then men attached two heavier lines to the thin one and the men on the boat started to pull them across – but as she watched she wondered how the people on the boat would use them to get to safety. Would they become tightrope walkers like she'd seen at the circus? She shivered at the thought of falling off into the sea. Then the men attached the two strong ropes to the sides of a buoy: Eliza could just make out something hanging below it. As the men pulled it across she worked out that people could climb into the middle of the buoy and then when she saw it being pulled back to shore with someone inside it she realised that what she had seen hanging underneath was a pair of breeches: these stopped the person falling through the hole into the sea. She was amazed at it, relieved as more and more people were pulled across, and very thankful that she was not on the ship. One by one people from the boat were pulled to safety above the waves.

'I'm cold,' said Mary, Richard's mother. 'Let's go.' Mary-Ann nodded as she linked arms with the older woman. They moved off along the side of the Bath Hotel and into St George's Road, followed by the rest of the group.

The following morning breakfast was suddenly interrupted by a loud banging at the door. When Henry opened it a man in a smart uniform said, 'Please sign here,' before giving Henry a brown envelope. Henry shut the door and turned round to see everyone frozen as if by a spell. He chuckled as he opened the telegram. Inside it said, 'River steamer 3.30 today, Southtown.' He turned it over and on the outside was a stamp from Yorkshire.

'My sister Mary and her family are arriving at 3.30 this afternoon,' he stated.

Henry met them from the paddle steamer which went up the river Yare between Norwich and Yarmouth. He recognised Mary immediately. He held her shoulders in his hands and they both smiled at each other. She turned to introduce her husband. As a couple they looked peculiar: Mary, at five feet seven inches, was taller than most women of her time and nearly as tall as her brother whereas her husband barely came up to her shoulder. Before she spoke the eyes of the two men met.

'This is Christmas,' Mary said. Henry smiled as he leant down to take the man's hand: Christmas was clean-shaven. 'And here are my children,' Mary continued, 'Alfred,' a serious young man bowed slightly towards him, 'and Mary-Ann, my daughter.' She was almost as tall as her father and coloured slightly when Henry took her gloved hand and kissed it.

By the time they reached Francis Buildings Tom and Eliza were home from school. Eliza's eyes flicked from one person to another in the room as she observed this new part of her family. She sensed the magnitude of her father's pleasure as he, now that they were indoors, hugged his sister closely; then he introduced her. Eliza examined her new aunt and could see that she was her father's sister: her hair was dark and straight like Henry's, she had large ears and both their eyes crinkled when they were smiling and laughing but then looked sad when they stopped – like they did now. Eliza heard her name and Henry noticed her frown.

'We were talking about my other sister,' he explained. 'She was called Eliza, like you, and died when you were a baby. That's why you were called Eliza,' he looked at her, 'and you still have Eliza's small, pointed chin.' He turned Eliza's head towards his sister to show her.

'Hello Eliza,' her aunt said, 'this is my daughter Mary-Ann.' Eliza looked at the other girl and wondered how old she was: she was about the same height as herself, perhaps just a little taller, but her skirt was as long as her mother's, reaching to the floor, and Eliza guessed that she was older. Aunt Mary introduced her son Alfred and Eliza noticed the cheeky grins that he and Tom exchanged and smiled to herself in anticipation of some fun while he was here.

Harry and William came in from work and were introduced. Eliza noticed her older brother talk confidently with the other adults while William hovered.

'Did they work you very hard at the ironworks today?' she asked him quietly so as not to interrupt the adults.

'Don't want to speak to you,' he grumped, 'but the adults are ignoring me. Yes, very hard. It's difficult because Mr Smithson won't let Harry near the hot metal yet so the rest of us are doing more. I don't like being near it myself.'

Eliza nodded and guessed that he was scared of getting hurt. 'You've only just started your training. I'm sure you'll be more confident when you know more. You're very strong.' William smiled at Eliza and she beamed back happily: it didn't happen often.

'I wonder what our new uncle's called,' he said. Alfred heard him and grinned. His sister, Mary-Ann, looked irritated.

'He's called Christmas,' said Alfred with a glance at his father. William, Tom and Eliza all laughed. Christmas came over to them. Mary, noticing him move, turned round to the children.

'I'm sorry I forgot to introduce your uncle.'

'Yes. I'm Uncle Christmas,' he said as he looked around them and they all laughed again. Eliza thought he was as jolly as Father Christmas should be but was slightly disappointed because he had no beard. She realised that, even though she was only eight, she wasn't that much smaller than he was.

Mary-Ann looked at him. 'Oh Pa, it's really not that funny.'

'It is to us,' retorted Tom. Mary-Ann scowled. He turned to Christmas; 'I'm Tom.'

'And I'm Eliza,' Eliza added and then continued, 'So that means we have Uncle Christmas and Aunt Mary.' The rest of the adults had stopped talking.

'And we have an Aunt Mary and Uncle Henry,' said Alfred.

Harry laughed. 'It's going to get very confusing at the celebration because we have another Aunt Mary at the yard!'

Well I can help with that,' Mary smiled, 'people sometimes call me Mary Christmas so I can be your Aunt Mary Christmas.' Everyone, with the exception of Mary-Ann, started saying, 'Aunt Mary Christmas,' to each other, all at once. When the clamour had died down Henry's wife turned to the young girl who seemed discomfited

'And I'm really Mary-Ann like you,' she said to the her, 'so you could call me Aunt Mary-Ann.' The young Mary-Ann nodded hesitantly at the older one, only smiling after the older Mary-Ann had smiled first. Eliza wondered how easy it was going to be, as her new cousin would be sleeping in the other bed in her side of the room. Tom started talking to Alfred and then moved round the table to where Eliza was standing; she joined in with the two boys. William and the young Mary-Ann, neither of them having the confidence to talk to the adults, were left standing looking at each other. Tom, Eliza and Alfred were close in age and chatted easily. While she was talking Eliza could see William at the edge of her vision. She saw Mary-Ann move closer to him and start talking; before long William was smiling and talking a lot. Eliza felt resentful of her cousin who could so easily make her brother smile.

On the day after they arrived, which was Friday, Henry allowed Eliza and Tom to take the day off school so they could take their cousins to see the town. The two mothers, Mary-Ann and Mary Christmas had been invited, along with Elizabeth, wife of Robert the miller, to visit Freddie's wife Ruth.

'What am I to do?' pondered Christmas, aloud, after the other men had left for their day's work at the yards. 'Could I come out with you to see the town?' he asked the children. 'I'll meet the rest of the family at the celebration.' For a moment Eliza was disappointed because she'd been looking forward to a day without adult supervision but she was also amazed at the novelty of an adult asking children for permission. She looked at his hopeful face and then at the two boys; they all nodded.

'Actually I'd rather not walk round all day. Can I come with you and Aunt Mary-Ann?' Mary-Ann asked her mother. Eliza stiffened. She looked at her mother who guessed what she was thinking. Then the young Mary-Ann continued, 'I don't need Eliza to come with me if she would rather go out.' Eliza was relieved and gave her cousin a grateful smile which was returned. Eliza had tried to befriend Mary-Ann but her cousin was five years older than she was: they were very different from one another and, whilst they were polite, they would never be the best of friends.

Before they left Eliza's mother had warned her to act like a young lady and, while usually she would have ignored that instruction, she complied. Her father was happy, and when her father was happy her mother lost her frown: Eliza didn't want to spoil it. Besides, Uncle Christmas had offered her his arm as they left the house and it made her feel very grown-up: Christmas was just the right height for her to hold his arm properly, like Ma did Pa's, not up in the air like she needed to do with most adults.

'Alfred wants to go down to the beach first,' shouted Tom as he led him down Northgate towards the town. The two boys raced ahead of Christmas and Eliza.

'Alfred's excited because he's never seen t'sea before and so am I really,' said Christmas. 'I 'aven't seen the sea since I were a lad meself.'

'I can't imagine living away from the sea,' replied Eliza. 'I like to watch the waves when it's rough - and I like it when it's still and the sky is blue and it seems as if you can see to the end of the world. It's no wonder people used to think the earth was flat.' Eventually they reached the boys who had waited near St Nicholas' church and looked very impatient.

'Is there somewhere we can meet if you boys don't want to keep waitin' for us?' asked Christmas.

Tom looked at Eliza. 'By the Britannia Pier gates?' Eliza nodded and then laughed when the boys raced off again. When Eliza and Christmas reached the pier the boys were already playing on the sand.

'Shall we walk along Marine Drive?' suggested Eliza. Tom pulled a face and Alfred looked disappointed.

'I think they want t'stay on t'beach,' said Christmas. Tom started to take off his shoes and roll up his breeches.

'What are you doing?' Alfred asked.

'I'm going to paddle – walk in the sea,' Tom explained to a perplexed Alfred, 'I don't want to get my breeches wet.'

Eliza was happy to watch them and started to walk along the promenade with Christmas. 'The boys can walk along the sand while we walk on here,' she suggested and as soon as she'd spoken the boys ran towards the sea. After a few minutes Christmas suggested they joined the boys.

'I'm not sure. You see Ma told me I had to remember I was a young lady and I don't think young ladies paddle,' she explained.

Christmas laughed. 'But you are a very young, young lady.'

'I-I may fall over or the waves may splash me. I d-don't want father to be upset,' she replied.

'If you hold onto me arm you can't fall and if you get wet it'll dry before we reach 'ome. I'd like to and I'm your guest so, as a young lady, t'would be impolite of you t'refuse.' His eyes sparkled and he grinned at Eliza's delight.

They walked south along the beach, paddling as they went, until they came level with Nelson's column. Then they left the beach and sat on the wall round the monument while their feet dried, eating the bread which they'd brought with them.

'It can't be Nelson's column,' declared Alfred, 'that's a lady at the top.'

'It's Britannia,' Tom informed him, 'You know, "Rule, Britannia!" like the song,' but Alfred still looked puzzled.

'Don't you sing it in school?' Eliza asked. Alfred shook his head and Eliza sang a line from the chorus.

Uncle Christmas's face lit up in recognition. 'I've heard it but we live inland whereas you live in a town where the sea is important. I expect you sing it a lot.' Tom and Eliza nodded unenthusiastically. 'But why is she looking towards the land? I thought Nelson was a sailor.'

'He was,' agreed Tom. 'According to Mr Mounseer at school he was in the Navy and defeated the French which makes him the best Englishman ever. It's pointing towards where he was born.' He looked at Eliza.

'Burnam I think,' she filled in.

They walked back along South Quay and up Fuller's Hill, meeting up with Henry on Northgate as he came out of the yard. Eliza noticed his smile of satisfaction at seeing her walking along with Christmas rather than running about with the boys.

When they arrived home Mary-Ann was sitting by the fire while the two mothers were preparing food. Eliza felt she had had a wonderful day and thought how dull her cousin seemed, so she ignored her and went through to the kitchen.

'Do you want me to help?' she asked. Mary Christmas shook her head.

'You could ask Tom and Alfred to go for water,' her mother suggested. Eliza picked up the empty bucket and took it through to the boys. Harry and William were just coming in from work. Mary-Ann and William exchanged glances as she jumped up from her seat: she had come to life and Eliza guessed why.

12

Henry's grandfather Thomas Spandler, who had started the millwright's yard at the beginning of the nineteenth century, had built an arcade from the wall of the workshop building along the length of the yard; its roof was tiled and the pillars were of oak, now darkening as years elapsed. It was where the lathes, planes, saws, and drills, powered by Bessie the steam engine, were kept, so that they could be operated in all but the worst of weather. For the birthday celebration these tools had been moved back to create a space under the roof for the tables of food. The furnace, in the previous twenty-four hours, had been used to roast meat and since mid-afternoon the potato spits had been in continuous use: the cooked potatoes were kept warm stored in a metal crate in Bessie's side of the furnace which had been cleared of ash. The yard had been thoroughly swept to remove wood-shavings and sawdust before several free-standing braziers had been lit and positioned along the wall under the arcade. Each family had brought as many lanterns as they could find and these, together with those that the children had made from hollowed-out turnips, were lit as the evening went dark. Apples were dangling on lengths of string from the arcade roof and floating in a barrel of water: these were customs that were part of celebrations in years when the harvest brought more food than people could eat and would, by the end of that century, become associated with the eve of All Saints' Day. To Eliza it seemed as though the yard had become a magical space.

In front of the cottage a large awning had been erected for the musicians. Her cousins Hannah and Susan hadn't arrived yet so Eliza was sitting on her own in a corner. She was watching the musicians nearby: one was tapping out a rhythm on a small drum; another was sitting infront of a case and hitting strings on it with two spoon-like hammers; a third was squeezing together what looked like a strangely-shaped pair of bellows and changing the sound by pressing buttons on the side and the last was bowing a fiddle energetically. Eliza's senses took in the sights and sounds and for a time these cut her off from her surroundings. Eventually she became aware that someone was looking at her. She looked away from the musicians to see Aunt Hannah sitting on her own. Their eyes met and the old lady smiled. Eliza decided to go and talk to her.

'Hello, you seem to be happy,' she said and smiled, which offset her plainness. Aunt Hannah returned the smile as she ran her finger down Eliza's nose until she reached the tip; she patted her cheek.

'Hello – you're Henry's youngest, aren't you?'

'Yes, my name is Eliza,' she replied, 'I'm eight.'

'I remember when I was eight,' she mused, 'and I came here for the first time. I remember my father and my older brothers standing in a group talking loudly and pointing here and there. This was just a big open space with nothing in it then: my mother took us girls into the cottage after a few minutes.' Her eyes gleamed. 'That was where we were going to live and we went into each of the rooms. We were so excited!' Hannah was talking quite loudly and there was a patch of red on both her cheeks. Her older brother's widow, Susanna, approached, smiling.

'You're enjoying your celebration?'

Hannah nodded. 'I'm becoming acquainted with this young lady.' Susanna frowned. 'It's Eliza, she's our Henry's granddaughter,' Hannah explained, 'and her father is young Henry.' Eliza chuckled and both of the women turned towards her.

'I think my brother must be young Henry now – my father is old!' she exclaimed. They were all laughing when Edmund approached.

He scowled at Eliza. 'Go back with the children, girl,' he ordered and Eliza scurried away. He turned to Hannah who had stopped smiling. 'I hope my yard meets with your expectations for your birthday. I must say it looks very different from its usual place of work.'

'It does Edmund.' The tightness of her lips indicated her disapproval. 'That was Henry's girl whom you frightened,' Edmund smirked, 'and I was enjoying talking with her.' He nodded curtly, turned and walked away. Mary, his mother, had been watching; she joined them.

'What happened then?' she asked.

'I was talking to young Eliza. Edmund ordered her away and then asked me if the yard was alright for me. I told him that I'd been enjoying talking with Eliza and he just nodded and walked away. No manners.'

'He's still resentful,' Mary explained. 'The way his father left this place to him and yet still left him powerless – perhaps I was wrong but I didn't even ask him about this celebration, just spoke to young Henry and he organised the pattern of work so that they cleared everything away yester..' She stopped, puzzled: her sisters-in-law were laughing again.

'Eliza – she said that if we say young Henry we must mean her brother – her father is old!' Mary was the first to stop laughing.

'I don't know what to do about Edmund.' She shook her head. 'He has no interest in the yard except to exert his authority when it suits him. He doesn't mix with the men and he doesn't care. Henry, however, is as good at running the yard as my Robert thought he would be. Look at Edmund now.' He was standing on the edge of a group of men which included Henry, Freddie, Robert the miller and Richard from London, all of them Edmund's cousins; he wasn't talking to any of them.

'He looks like a fox observing his prey,' suggested Hannah. 'He's not even following the conversation but staring closely at each of them in turn. How strange.' The band's tempo changed and there was a roar of laughter from the group as they moved into the centre of the room and started to dance. Edmund startled as if they'd suddenly shouted at him. Eliza, who was watching her father dancing and laughing with the other men, had noticed that the unpleasant man who had ordered her away was standing gawping at them. After a few moments he sat down rather heavily on a stool; his mouth was open; his sweaty forehead reflected the candlelight and he did not look happy. Eliza wondered who he was.

Ruth and Elizabeth, wives of Freddie and Robert the miller, arrived with their children. Eliza was glad to see Hannah and Susan and they were given charge of the younger ones which included some whom the girls did not know, children of Henry's cousins who did not live in Yarmouth as well as Hannah's younger sisters Emily and Elizabeth. A temporary pen had been erected in which the older girls could keep them safe. On the serving tables, as well as the meat and potatoes which had cooked on the spit, there was a selection of fruit drinks for the children which Hannah's mother had made and some bread and large cakes baked by Elizabeth. Nobody minded how often the three older girls went back for more food as long as the younger ones were kept happy.

Eliza saw William and he looked very happy: he was with their cousin Mary-Ann. Tom and Alfred approached them. William said something to Mary-Ann and they both laughed; the younger boys both left. Although she was glad to see her brother so happy she was disconcerted by it. Suddenly her thoughts were interrupted when everyone started laughing. She looked towards the centre of the yard at Freddie and Christmas. Together they made people laugh even when they were just standing together: Freddie was such a large, tall man and Christmas was like a gnome beside him. The band had started a jig and when they danced they were very funny: they kept falling over and helping each other up. Sometimes they moved together but Christmas had to take three steps to Freddie's two making everyone laugh. When they came together in a dance and tried to clap Freddie nearly fell over Christmas because his hand went through the air above his head while Christmas winded him by clapping into his stomach. Of course, the more people laughed, the more they exaggerated and the sillier they became. When Freddie came near the audience he pulled faces which made his scars move around his face. Many people were crying with laughter and begging them to stop.

The evening soon passed and it was late. The young children had fallen asleep in their pen. Eliza was tired. Then the music stopped. Hannah, Mary and Susanna walked into the centre. Everyone went quiet as Hannah began to speak.

'It's been a wonderful evening. I want to thank everyone for coming. I'm sure my father would be amazed if he could see you all, his descendants. My brothers would be happy that you have all come. Thank you again.' Everyone clapped.

Eliza couldn't believe the evening was over. Tomorrow everyone would be travelling back to their own homes. She would miss Uncle Christmas and she knew her father would miss his sister.

They arrived back at Francis buildings; everyone was glum.

'I don't want you to go,' declared William.

'None of us do,' said Henry, looking round the room; William, however, only looked at his cousin; Eliza noticed.

13

The following morning Henry, Harry, William, Tom and Eliza all accompanied Christmas, Mary and their children to the railway station. Although they had arrived on the river steamer from Norwich because Mary had wanted to see the Norfolk countryside again, they were returning by train because it was quicker. They had to be sure of catching the early train northwards at Norwich: there were several connections they needed to make that day before they would reach the station at Richmond, in Yorkshire, near where they lived. The millwrights who employed Christmas had given him leave of a day and a half at the end of the previous week and he wanted to be sure he was back for Monday morning. Henry walked with his sister; they spoke but did not smile. Christmas and Harry followed them; they were having a discussion about brass with which Smithson's, the foundry where Harry worked, had recently started working. Behind them William and Mary-Ann walked together talking quietly and looking at each other frequently. Only Alfred, Tom and Eliza were not downcast. With the gaiety of children they chatted as they enjoyed the walk through the autumn sunshine, the many stones and shells from the beach that Alfred was taking home in his pockets making Tom and Eliza chuckle.

As the train moved away Henry stared at his sister through the glassless windows of the old second-class carriage whilst she huddled down next to Christmas; he did not wave. The train left in a cloud of smoke and steam and they turned for home. Henry wanted to walk alone but Harry and William walked with him and when his pace slowed as they neared the King's Arms Harry quickly asked him something about the properties of brass. Henry liked to show his knowledge and thus they all returned to Francis buildings together. Mary-Ann served up a boiled bacon and mash dinner which was eaten in silence. Henry looked at no-one, diligently applying himself to the food on his plate.

They were just finishing when the door opened and Carrie walked in because it was Sunday and she had the afternoon off. As usual she smiled broadly at the sight of her family.

'Hello..' she began but faltered at the aura of gloom.

'Hello Carrie,' said Mary-Ann. 'Everyone has gone home.'

'But I'm here now. You must tell me all about the celebration. Was there dancing?' Mary-Ann and Eliza started describing the previous evening. After a few minutes Henry pulled on his coat and left. As the door closed Harry looked at William. William's eyes flicked from his brother to the door and back; he nodded and they followed their father. Tom also left: he was still doing some work for Mr Greensome, deep digging in part of the nursery that hadn't been used that season.

'I'm glad to take off that corset,' said Carrie when all the men had left. 'Have to wear it all the time except when I'm in bed.' Her frown dissolved into a smile. 'It's good to be home. Next week Mr Olivito and his family are going to Italy. Then the week after we need to clean thoroughly in the way that you can't do when they're there.' Mary-Ann and Eliza nodded their understanding. 'After that I'll be home until the week after Easter.'

'The baby doesn't show too much even without your corset. You're doing well,' commented Mary-Ann.

'What will you do when you come home?' Eliza asked.

Carrie shrugged. 'Help mother I suppose.'

'I do the kitchen and clean this room on Saturdays, including the fires,' Eliza informed her. Mary-Ann smiled at her youngest daughter before turning back to Carrie.

'I think you should stick to the mending, then you can sit down,' she suggested.

'What about the market? Could I not do some of the shopping? It's cold now so with my big coat on no one will know.'

Eliza frowned. 'Why must no one know? I'm excited that there's a baby inside you whom we'll see soon.'

Carrie looked irritated. 'Remember I explained before I went away.'

'Yes, but it's not your fault,' Eliza persisted, 'you didn't want that man to attack you.'

'People just think a woman who's pregnant without a man to support her is wrong.'

'That's not fair.'

'That's how it is Eliza. If this happens,' she jerked a thumb at her rounded belly, 'it's the woman's fault. Men just do it. I was wrong because I was on my own. It's like I was saying I wanted him to rape me.'

'But you didn't!' Eliza exclaimed.

'Yes, I suppose it wouldn't do you any harm to go shopping,' agreed Mary-Ann, ignoring Eliza's questions. Blinking rapidly, Carrie turned to her mother.

'Couldn't just sit here sewing all day.' The pitch of her voice was higher than usual. 'Doing a bit of shopping won't hurt me. Last week I was turning beds.'

Mary-Ann frowned. 'I suppose with being so tall it wouldn't have been such a strain for you. I remember I was lifting bales of hay on the farm when I was pregnant with Louisa before I told my mother. She soon stopped me from doing heavy work when she knew. It's a dangerous time being pregnant.' Silence extinguished the conversation. Eliza's eyes were wide. She'd had friends whose mothers had died giving birth so that they'd had to leave school to look after their younger siblings. She hadn't thought that Carrie might die. She hugged her big sister and looked into her eyes. Carrie ran her fingers through Eliza's hair and smiled. Eliza was still discomforted but she was happy that Carrie was coming home soon.

'Well I don't think this Saturday will be as exciting as the last one,' remarked Tom as he and Eliza walked home from school the following Thursday. 'I miss having Alfred here – he was fun to be with!'

'Yes, but I'm quite pleased that I no longer have Mary-Ann in my room. She was strange. Far to grown-up and serious for me.'

'William seemed to like her.'

'Two strange ones together. He's going to the bedroom early each evening. What's he doing?'

Tom shrugged. 'Writing something as far as I can tell.'

'Perhaps he's started keeping a diary,' suggested Eliza. Tom pulled a face. 'Or,' Eliza's thoughts tumbled out, 'maybe he's writing a letter?'

Tom looked amazed. 'Mary-Ann?'

Eliza nodded. 'Whatever it is it seems to have improved his temper.'

Tom suddenly changed the subject. 'Did I tell you about John Harris?' Eliza shook her head. 'I found out at the end of last week. With all the excitement I forgot. He's not been in school this term and apparently he's not coming back.'

'Why not?'

'He's working. His father bought that old bakery on Horse Plain years ago to use as a kiln for firing pipes. Apparently there was another pipe making business on Row fifty-one and now he's taken over that. He wants his son to work it for him.'

'What a pity – I remember you saying he was very clever. He must be disappointed to leave school.'

'Not at all,' Tom scoffed, 'he'd always helped his father and became excited every time he spoke about the pipe-making. Yes, he is very clever and I'm sure he'll use his brain in the business – and make a good deal of money!'

'I'm not looking forward to when I have to finish school. I love learning things – although I enjoyed selling the radishes. Trouble is when I leave school it'll be so that I can "be a good woman" as Pa keeps saying. It'll be tedious.'

'Yes but think how dangerous it is to be a man. Remember Harry's finger.'

'A man can at least use his skill to keep himself safe,' countered Eliza. 'A woman will have babies and risks dying each time. That frightens me.' Momentarily she was silent. 'And then the rest of the time my life will be dull.' Tom looked sideways at his sister and shrugged his shoulders. They reached Francis Buildings.

Eliza went straight through to the kitchen where Mary-Ann was preparing dinner. 'What do you need help with?' she asked.

'Do you not have schoolwork to finish?'

Eliza shook her head. 'I finished in class – I seem to find the work easier than the other girls.'

'Then you can clean those carrots.' Mary-Ann turned back to where she was gutting some fish, her face a frown, while Eliza went upstairs to change into her house dress. The front door slammed: Tom had gone to the nursery.

Later that evening Henry and Tom were sitting on the floor. The tongues in both Tom's boots had torn from their place and Henry thought it was time Tom learnt how to use a cobbler's needle with its complex system of upper and lower threads, one on a spool and the other wrapped round the fingers to keep it under tension. They each had a boot and Tom was trying hard to copy his father. It was difficult.

'There's not much room in here,' complained Tom.

'There's even less for me,' said Henry, holding up his large hand. They worked on without speaking for a while.

'Pa, John Harris has left school. He is younger than me -.'

'– Younger than I am,' corrected Henry.

Tom drew a deep breath. 'I'd like to work full time at the nursery.'

Henry put down the boot. 'No Tom. You need your schooling if you want to be free to choose an apprenticeship. Most masters expect lads to know more than you do now. You won't rise above a labourer without more education.'

'Since I went up to the senior school we learn geometry and algebra, not just arithmetic, and I find it hard to understand.' He paused. 'Mr Greensome has told me that he would take me on.'

'No Tom. Work hard at your mathematics and apply yourself then you will understand. I think that perhaps you need to give up your work at the nursery during term time. Then you can concentrate on your studies.'

'But Pa -.'

'No Tom. Do not speak of it again. Go to the nursery tomorrow but tell Mr Greensome that you cannot continue.' Tom pushed his lips together and jammed his needle into the leather of his boot.'

The following morning on the way to school Tom expressed his frustration.

'Mathematics is so hard to understand. Father tells me that all I need to do is work and apply myself but I just don't want to. I'm sick of books. I want to go to work not school: I'm nearly as tall as Father and I want to be paid for my time.'

Eliza didn't answer because she knew her brother and knew that when he made up his mind arguing with him was like trying to blow the wind back into the sky; his comments put her mind into a whirl.

The master has been doing mathematics with a group of boys who are going to the seniors next term – he allowed me to listen and I understood easily. I've already finished the arithmetic at the lower school. I know that when I move up I won't do mathematics – because I'm a girl. We'll be taught simple reckoning – again – so that we can double recipes and check our change when we go shopping but I can do all of that now. Tom is exasperating! If only I was a boy.

The year turned and Carrie grew bigger. Henry confined her to the house but at the end of the first week in January there was such a heavy fall of snow that she wouldn't have ventured out anyway. On the twenty-fourth of January the child was born. Eliza lay awake in bed that night listening to the funny little new-born baby sounds. She smiled in delight. The following morning she held him for the first time and quivered with excitement: this tiny, living person opened her young heart and she loved him.

Two weeks went by and Eliza had become used to James, as he was called, being in her room. Now she ignored the sounds he made at night and hoped he wouldn't wake up: he usually did and his cries always woke her although she didn't mind too much and went back to sleep as soon as he started sucking. At first Carrie had kept him to herself but now, having the care of him all day, she was happy to let Eliza have him after school while she helped Mary-Ann with the evening meal.

Later that evening Henry and Harry had gone out. Mary-Ann and Carrie were on the chairs near the fire, murmuring to each other, sewing. Tom was sitting on one of the benches at the table studying and Eliza was opposite him: on the table was a mortar containing an infusion of sage with which she was bathing the baby's head to try and ease the cradle-cap on his scalp. William was upstairs but then they heard him come down the stairs and go out to the yard. A while later he came back but instead of going upstairs again he came through the door into the living room. He sat down at the table next to Eliza and watched her intently.

'Carrie, when Eliza's finished can I hold James?' Carrie stiffened and Mary-Ann put a hand on her knee. 'I'll be really careful,' he urged. He put his thumb into the baby's palm and James grasped it tightly; then he stroked the small hand with one of his large fingers. He looked at Eliza and smiled. She was delighted by the warmth and pleasure she felt coming from her brother. She looked over to Carrie. Carrie's eyes met William's and after a moment she nodded.

'Ma, should I dry James's head?' Eliza asked.

'No, it would be good for the sage water to stay on his head as long as possible. It will dry up anyway then it can be washed off in the morning. He shouldn't get cold in here.'

Eliza turned to William with the baby. He held out his arms.

'You know he's not strong enough to hold his own head up?'

He nodded. 'I do now that you've told me.' Carrie had stopped sewing. Her lips were slightly apart and two small patches of colour appeared on her cheeks as she watched. After a few moments she breathed normally. William sat perfectly still, staring at James. Then he lifted him towards his face. Carrie tensed again but Eliza was calm: she could sense how happy William was. He kissed James and Eliza reached to him and squeezed his arm.

Mary-Ann looked from Carrie to her other children and grandson at the table; she sighed audibly and William looked at her. Eliza felt as if they were all wrapped in a huge woolly scarf.

'What happened last night?' Tom asked as they walked to school the following morning. 'I couldn't work it out. William was acting strangely and everyone was smiling a lot.'

'You know how hard and cross he usually is?' Tom nodded. 'Did you see how gentle he was with James? It was as if he'd lost all his anger.'

Tom was unconvinced. 'Yes, well let's see what he's like the next time someone upsets him. Then we'll know if there's really been a change.'

'Ma's happy, and so am I,' Eliza continued, 'but I'm also thinking about what's made him change.' Tom peered at her but then smiled knowingly.

'I think I know but I can't tell you. I said I'd keep it secret. He doesn't want Pa to know yet.'

'It's Mary-Ann isn't it? I was right wasn't I?' Eliza could see the truth in Tom's face. 'He's writing to her isn't he? Don't worry I won't tell Pa or anyone else. Why does he want to hide it?'

'He thinks Pa will write to Uncle Christmas and that they'll stop them.'

'I haven't seen any letters arrive.' She glanced at the front door.

'No they're sending the letters to the post office and collecting them themselves. He says he plans to tell Pa in time. He thinks Pa will make a big fuss so I suppose he's waiting in case she stops writing.'

'Well I hope she carries on because it makes him happy and that's easier for the rest of us. I'm sure Pa is bound to notice him though, he's just so different. I wouldn't be surprised if Ma tells him about last night.' She frowned. 'I hope it comes right for him.' Eliza had just reached the junior girls' entrance. She turned in as the senior bell sounded and Tom broke into a run.

14

Carrie and Eliza were in the kitchen helping Mary-Ann, Tom was writing at the table and James was asleep in the cradle next to his grandfather. Harry and William had only just returned from Smithson's and were warming themselves by the fire. Henry put down his paper and bent down and stroked his grandson, his rough finger causing the baby's cheek to twitch. He looked up at his sons; his habitual frown was absent.

'It's going to be a hard frost tonight,' suggested Harry.

'Yes, February, you expect that,' replied William, 'although it'll be Lent soon and that means spring isn't too far away.'

Henry laughed. 'It's still the middle of winter.' Harry and William turned to look at him. 'There's at least two more weeks to go before Shrove Tuesday. Then we have to have the whole of Lent before spring is close.'

William turned to his father and grinned. 'But by the end of Lent there'll be crocuses and the birds will be singing. When I was walking through Market Place I noticed snowdrops already on the windowsills of the Angel Inn. And the days are lengthening.' He bounded over to the window just as Eliza came through from the kitchen. The sight of his animation arrested her movement; she smiled. Tom quickly moved his schoolbooks from the table as she put down a bowl of steaming potatoes.

'Did I hear you say Shrove Tuesday? Are we going to the fair?' she asked, knowing that they would.

Yarmouth's Orange Fair was held on Shrove Tuesday which in 1860 fell on the twenty-first of February. The townsfolk looked forward to it during the bleakness of the winter: there would be games designed to extract money with little reward but the excitement of possible, but improbable, winnings and unusual things to look at such as a wild, spitting cat in a cage, or a man with a grotesque nose, on show for a fee. It was all very entertaining after their own firesides. Usually there was only one ride: it was old, comprising of dobby horses fixed to a circular board. These horses had been made from lengths of tree trunk into which a groove had been cut from which a head, made from a piece of wooden board, protruded; strips of rabbit-skin represented a mane and tail and the legs were short, chunky sticks. Underneath there was a cranking mechanism which enabled the roundabout to be turned at speeds which excited the children.

This fair had always been a trade fair, unlike the fair on the Friday after Easter, but of recent years there were fewer and fewer trade stalls so that Spandler's had decided not to have one this year: their order books were full and consequently both of their young apprentices were fully occupied. Smithson's, however, sent Harry and William with a selection of tools and novelty gadgets to sell, in fact anything that they thought people might buy and could be made at their yard.

'Pa's right because the trade stalls are only down this side of Market Place. There's none over there this year,' observed Harry, nodding his head towards the fishermen's hospital.

'Yes. All the stalls this side aren't trade either,' added William. 'The animals are down towards the Angel. I saw one of the keepers struggling out of the door with a huge pail of water earlier.'

'Johnny at the Angel's clever. I expect he asked for them to be there because people stand around looking at the animals. You can be sure there'll be some savoury smells wafting out to entice customers in.'

William pivoted round, his eyes moving over the fair. 'Two rides this year! Looking forward to going on those swings. We'll make them fly!' He grinned.

As well as the dobby horses there were swing boats. Each boat could take four people and swung from an iron frame. At the top of the frame three horizontal poles were positioned above the boats from the ends of which stout ropes hung. These were crossed so that the passengers pulled alternately on the end of the pole opposite to where they were seated and thus caused the boat to swing.

At Francis Buildings Tom and Eliza came in from school.

'Ma, when we've changed can we go up to the fair?' Tom asked.

Mary-Ann nodded. 'Put your second-best dress on, Eliza, and remember Pa and I will come later.' It was her mother's way of reminding Eliza to be a young lady and Eliza scowled although she couldn't stay cross for long because she was too excited.

They approached the fair along Northgate and as they walked past the tall railings around the west end of St Nicholas' graveyard they could see into Church Plain.

'Look there's a new ride!' shouted Tom.

'Swings,' observed Eliza, quickening her pace. However, when she reached them she realised how big they were.

'I could pull one end,' suggested Tom hopefully but Eliza was shaking her head.

'I don't think I could pull hard enough on my own. Besides which we haven't any money.'

They turned to the dobby ride.

'Could I help turn, Mister?' Tom asked the man at the ride.

The man nodded. 'Turn for five runs of the pebbles and you can have a free go, young sir.' Two large, metal ovoids were joined together and mounted in a frame. One was full of small pebbles and when the ride started the man inverted the ovoids so that the pebbles could be heard falling into the empty one. When all the pebbles had fallen the sound stopped and that signalled the end of the ride. Eliza stood and watched, wishing she could have a go at turning but knowing that the man would not let her.

She was losing interest in what she could see when she noticed Ruth, Freddie's wife, approaching with the pram, surrounded by the girls. She waved and Hannah and Emily ran over towards her. A few moments later Ruth, with Elizabeth holding onto the pram, caught up with them. Eliza leaned over, peeped in and smiled at baby James. She chuckled to herself because it amused her that he had the same name as Carrie's baby.

'Ma, can we go on the dobbies?' asked Hannah whilst Emily bounced up and down beside her.

'Yes but you can have Betsy on your dobby and Emily can ride with Eliza.' Emily pulled a face. 'It's either that or not go on the dobby at all Emily. I still think you need to have someone hold onto you, if that's all right with Eliza?'

Eliza nodded happily: she was earning her ride and a lot more easily than Tom. She winked at him gleefully as she climbed on.

They finished on the ride and watched Tom have his turn. He was on his own and the man made the ride turn very fast for him. He leaned out from his horse and they all jumped back out of his way, laughing. Afterwards Ruth explained that she was going to meet Freddie from the yard and would see them later. As they left Tom and Eliza walked across the market square, scanning the stalls for their brothers.

'Over there!' Tom shouted. They noticed that some of the other trade stalls were packing away their goods.

'Do you want us to help pack up?' Eliza asked.

'Tom can,' replied Harry.

'And you can sit on our stool and be a young lady,' continued William with a grin. Eliza scowled but was really quite happy to sit and watch them working.

They finished. Harry and William argued over who was going to go down the Row to the yard to tell them they were ready: the cart would be too heavy for them to roll safely down the Row so some of the men would come and help. By the time they left Ruth and the children had returned with Freddie and Henry was with them.

'I'm just going to fetch Ma and then we can choose what to eat,' said Henry on his way past. The smells from the food stalls had been making Eliza's tummy rumble whilst she'd been watching the boys pack up and she hoped he wouldn't be long.

'A new ride I see,' said Freddie, his eyes twinkling, 'is it fun?'

'Don't know,' replied Tom. 'Eliza didn't think she could do one side on her own.'

'I don't think Pa would want me to do it at all,' muttered Eliza.

'Well Hannah wants to and I don't think she'll be able to do it on her own either so you're going to have to help her,' declared Freddie with a grin that made his scars move: Eliza couldn't help giggling but then she stopped. She didn't want to upset her father but she really wanted to go on the swing with Hannah. The decision was made for her when Freddie lifted her up and plonked her in the boat. It did feel wobbly! Freddie turned back for Hannah while Tom scrambled into the other side. Freddie made sure they had their ropes and then went behind the girls' end of the boat and heaved it along to start it off. Tom saw what was needed and pulled on his rope as it reached the top of its swing.

'Pull!' yelled Freddie as the girls' side reached its height, but he needn't have shouted. The girls had looked at each other as their side went up and reached up high on the rope so they could pull down, which they did at just the right moment. After a few minutes Eliza could feel herself becoming hot and sweaty with the exertion and knew that the wind created by their speed was loosening her bonnet and her hair was escaping. She didn't care: this was fun!

'My arms are hurting,' shouted Tom after a while.

'Keep going,' Hannah shouted back but after another three pulls Tom stopped.

'Aw, you stopped! Eliza yelled, laughing. The smile on her face froze as the swing-boat slowed down and she saw her father standing there. Freddie stepped forward and lifted the girls down. Eliza's bonnet was now all the way down the back of her head and her hair was awry, some of it sticking to her sweaty forehead. Mary-Ann quickly stepped forward to put it right.

Henry glared. 'I could hear you from fifty yards away,' he growled. 'You're all hot and red like some common labourer.'

Freddie beamed at Eliza. 'Thank-you for helping Hannah.'

Henry huffed. 'You're a young lady. Remember that!'

Freddie moved to stand close to Henry; he muttered in his ear. 'They're both girls, not yet in double figures. There'll be enough of acting properly when they're older.'

'She's my youngest,' Henry countered, 'and I made mistakes with the older two. She must marry well.'

'Marry!' Freddie guffawed. 'She's a child.'

'In a few years she'll have her own ideas if I don't train her now. She needs to accept the fact that I control her just as her husband will do in the future. She needs to conform so that I can make something of her.' He turned away from Freddie.

Make something of me!
Eliza's mind was in a whirl.

I'm me, not his thing that he can construct, like a mill. I don't want to be controlled, not now, not ever. When I marry I want it to be someone who will care for me not control me!'

Carrie, who had arrived with Mary-Ann and Henry, could see Eliza's consternation and put her arm round her sister's shoulder to steady her whilst Mary-Ann and Ruth looked at each other.

'We're all here now,' Ruth said in an unnaturally cheerful voice.

'Yes, let's find something to eat,' added Mary-Ann quickly. Henry shrugged and moved off in the direction of the food stalls.

The stalls, three of them, were grouped at right-angles to each other in the middle of the Market Place. This was where the Market Cross had stood, positioned on top of a large, hexagonal structure underneath which more than twenty people could gather. It was removed in 1836 and by 1860 the space left by the shelter had been filled with cobbles except for the hole where the central post had been. A large piece of heavy sailcloth covered the stalls and the space between them and was supported by a pole that had been driven into that hole. As the family entered Eliza was immediately buffeted by warm air. She shrugged her shoulders to dispel her irritation at her father and pulled Emily, whose hand she was holding, towards one of the benches.

'Come on, let's sit at this table.' All the girls shuffled along between the bench and the table and the boys sat opposite them. Ruth and Carrie sat next to the girls with their babies, Freddie having chained the pram to the outside of one of the stalls.

'Soup for them all, Dickie,' called out Freddie to the man on the stall.

'He looks like Humpty Dumpty,' muttered Tom to Eliza; she giggled and turned to look at the man who was indeed round and whose head was bald and shone in the candlelight. Richard Harris had known Freddie and Henry since they were both young boys. Normally they wouldn't buy soup in which unwholesome ingredients could be easily disguised, but they knew they could trust Dickie. Sometimes he didn't smell very pleasant because he worked in the Shambles abattoir behind the butchers' shops which fronted onto the Market Place opposite the Angel Inn but he had been a childhood friend of Freddie's and Henry's fathers. He remembered when Freddie nearly died from the burns to his face when he was two and was often Henry's salvation in the dark days of Henry's life after his father had left to seek his fortune.

They were all slurping the hot soup when a platter full of bread appeared before them. Henry looked up to see Mr Boulter standing there and he reached into his pocket for money but he shook his head.

'A gift,' he smiled but then he became more serious and lowered his voice. 'Louisa?' Henry and Mary-Ann looked at each other and shook their heads. There was no news. Mary-Ann had accepted that she would never know anything else about her eldest daughter: it was only when asked that she thought of her because it was less painful that way. Mr Boulter turned his attention to Carrie and Ruth.

'Two lovely babes, I see.' Ruth beamed; Carrie coloured and Henry pushed his lips together. Suddenly everyone was serious.

'Both of them are called James,' said Eliza with a chuckle. Eliza was aware of her father's frown but chose to look at all the other adults, who were laughing.

'Those bloaters smell good,' declared William as he drained the last of his soup. Freddie climbed out from between the bench and the table.

'Come and help me then,' he suggested and William followed him to the stall.

'You seem happy Will,' Freddie commented as they left the table. William grinned and nodded.

'Mr Smithson called me to his office yesterday. Said I was becoming skilled more quickly than any other apprentice he's ever had – and that includes Harry!'

'And how are you doing with your family?'

William stopped and turned to Freddie. He drew a deep breath and then spoke quickly. 'Eliza doesn't trust me – but I don't blame her. Ma and Carrie are also wary,' he was quiet for a moment, 'but Harry's fine.'

'Your Pa?'

'He's not happy.' Freddie frowned but William shook his head. 'Not because of me. He's been sad since his sister went home after Aunt Hannah's birthday.' They carried on towards the counter of the bloater stall.

'A dozen please,' Freddie asked the large red-headed lady behind the stall. They watched while she quickly gutted the herrings: Yarmouth bloaters were smoked whole. Warm oils oozed from them whilst she did it, making William's mouth water.

Eliza, Hannah and Emily laughed and chatted together as they slurped the fish from their fingers. Eliza helped Emily with her fish, showing her how to avoid the larger bones. As she ate she was aware that Pa and Freddie seemed to be talking rather urgently. She shivered.

As they came out from under the shelter they realised how cold it had become and they quickly left Market Place. Elizabeth was tired and Freddie picked her up. Emily was walking with Hannah and Eliza and they started falling behind.

'Come on girls, catch up,' called Tom. Hannah and Eliza pulled Emily between them and they joined the boys.

'It's Emily,' panted Hannah, 'she can't keep up.' Emily started to cry.

'Would you like a ride?' Harry asked and immediately the tears stopped. Harry swung her up onto his shoulders. As they approached Francis buildings Harry lifted her down and, refreshed, she skipped up to Freddie and Ruth.

Henry, Mary-Ann and Carrie had already gone inside.

15

Half an hour later Mary-Ann and Eliza brought tea through from the kitchen just as Carrie came down the stairs

'At last you're all here. I don't know why it takes you girls such a long time to do anything,' commented Henry, gruffly. 'I've things to say that are important.'

'James has fed well but was still awake when I left him. I may need to go back if he cries,' explained Carrie.

'You will not,' stated Henry. You'll stay here and listen. The child can cry.' No-one spoke. Henry slowly looked round the room. 'I have worked hard for many years. I wanted to make a good life for you all. The boys will be men and will look after themselves. Louisa's gone off with her sailor and we don't know where. Dead for all we know or living like a beggar.' Mary-Ann gasped but he didn't notice. 'Carrie you've got that babe but have no man to support you. Trouble is no one with any position will want you now so you'll probably be an old maid with a bastard till the end of your days. Mr Olivito's having you back?' She blinked the tears from her eyes and nodded. 'Good because you must always be that child's father as well as his mother and provide for him. I'm disappointed in you. I do not like people I know making a fuss of your babe – they look at me as if I'm a fool for keeping you in my family. And Eliza, I don't care what you want or feel. You must understand that I want the best for you, I want you to marry well. You will never again behave like you did tonight. Your Uncle Freddie may say you're just a child but you are nine and I plan that you will make a good marriage before you're fifteen.' Eliza's eyes opened wide and she felt as if her heart had stopped beating. 'You are my last chance to have a daughter of mine do well. In the next few years you will become the woman that men of money and position want.'

Eliza looked her father in the eye. 'W-what if I don't want to marry?'

'Don't be silly, Eliza.' Mary-Ann's voice was quiet and brusque. 'What else would you do?'

'Eliza you're a girl.' Henry's voice was quiet and even. 'Girls become women. They marry and have children. You have no choice.'

'But Pa..'

'No! Don't argue. That's how it will be!' Shouting now, his control gone, he banged the table and stood up. For a moment he stared at Eliza but then his gaze moved to the middle of the table. Wearily he drooped and shuffled to where his coat hung. Eliza felt as if the room was changing size, almost as if it was breathing; her vision misted and then shrunk to a small circle that encompassed the back of her father's head as it was eclipsed by the closing door. She felt her own heartbeat in the back of her neck; blackness descended and she fell to the floor. As soon as she fell she regained consciousness so that by the time Carrie had crossed the room to her she was sitting up.

An hour or so later Henry still hadn't returned and Harry left, telling Mary-Ann that he was going to look for his father. He found him in the King's Arms but it was too late: he was already displaying an alcoholic exuberance.

'Ale for my boy, barman,' he called as soon as he saw him. Harry sat down on the bench.

'Pa..'

'The fair wer good, my boy, wer is not? Did yer mek much money fer yews boss.' The alcohol had changed Henry's careful speech into common Norfolk. The barmaid came to them and placed a tankard in front of Harry; she turned to the table next to them, bending over to pick up some glasses. She had her back to Henry. He put his hand out and traced the shape of her bottom. He winked at Harry and then guffawed at the shock on his face. 'Sup yer drink then. It's good stuff,' he spluttered. A few more minutes went by during which Harry wished he'd gone for Freddie and wondered how he was going to stop his father having another drink. Just then the door swung open.

'Dickie!' yelled Henry and Harry remembered how cross he'd been because Eliza had shouted on the swing. He wondered if his father realised that he was standing out even above the shouts and laughter around them and that people were beginning to look at him and nudge each other. He was glad to see Dickie. Unfortunately Dickie came from the bar with a tray of three tankards. Henry, seeing him coming, downed the last of the one he was drinking.

'Good health!' Dickie exclaimed as he put down the tray. Henry leaned over the table and hugged him like a child, picking up his tankard and sloshing it as he sat down. The smile on Dickie's face froze and he looked across to Harry.

'Take no notice of Harry,' Henry said. 'Been sent by his Ma to mind me.' He took a huge gulp of his ale.

Dickie smiled. 'Seems like I need to help him then. Drink that slowly because you're not having any more.' Henry pulled a face. 'Do you want your son to carry you home?' Henry stared at him as if indignant but then slumped back against the wall. An hour later Harry and Dickie walked down Northgate to Francis buildings, supporting Henry between them.

At the house Eliza was near the fire balancing James on her knee whilst she changed his rags. She stopped and stared when the door opened and Harry and Dickie helped Henry to his chair; he slumped into it. James began to cry.

'Shut that bathtard.' Carrie quickly lifted James from Eliza's lap and took him upstairs.

'Whatth yew th-thtaring at?' Henry growled at William. 'Yewth a damaged man and no woman'll have yew.' William blanched and went to stand but Dickie put a hand on his shoulder.

'It's the ale,' he stated.

'Huh, yew've not theen him. Mek a woman ththcream it would.' Henry laughed. 'And he'th my th-thon.'

'She loves me so she'll accept me. She doesn't love my body,' William blurted out but then he caught the look of horror on Tom and Eliza's faces and stopped himself. 'She will, whoever falls in love with me,' he finished quickly – but Henry was too drunk to notice. William followed Carrie upstairs. Eliza, who had been watching his hands curl into fists, let go of the breath she'd been holding.

After Easter Carrie returned to work for Mr Olivito and baby James spent six weeks living with Freddie and Ruth. During that summer he started weaning and came home. However, although he was taking mushed up food from a spoon, he still needed to suckle. Ruth was quite happy to let him: she was young, strong and ate well so that the more the two babies sucked, the more milk she produced. Mid-morning Mary-Ann would walk up Caister Road to Vauxhall Gardens with James and the two women would enjoy each other's company; when Eliza came home from school she would take him back for his second feed. James was the first baby Eliza had had much contact with but the warm fuzziness she felt when she cuddled him she restricted, deliberately, to her emotions. She would not think about her future which included her father and the man he had ready for her to marry.

In September George, Freddie's brother, returned to Yarmouth. He had been living in London where his wife Jemima had given birth three times; only one baby lived and she was pregnant again. The two brothers were standing in Freddie's small front garden enjoying the afternoon sun when Henry walked up Vauxhall Gardens towards them.

'You remember George?' Freddie asked as Henry approached.

Henry nodded and turned to the tall, muscular man who bore a resemblance to the unscarred side of Freddie's face. 'You were at Robert's funeral. And, long before that, I can remember your christening! I was seventeen then. Your mother saw me looking at you and she passed you to me. You were so small. Everyone laughed because I was so clumsy – your mother quickly took you back!' The memory was from that carefree part of his life before his father left and Henry's eyes sparkled.

'I remember my father telling me that he hoped I turned out as well as you,' George replied. 'That was just before you married and I helped him wax the chairs he gave you. We worked on them together and he spoke about you a lot. Told me all about the troubles you'd had and how wonderful you were.'

Henry shook his head. 'It's such a pity he didn't tell me at the time. I've discovered since then that Uncle Robert thought the same. It would have made such a difference to have known.' He paused. 'Have you found work?'

George nodded. 'I'm under contract from the council to repair Nelson's monument. And in between I'm doing some casual work for Lacon's.'

'I can see how your training as a millwright would help at the top of the monument but Lacon's are a brewery. A millwright's job is thirsty work sometimes but how does drinking it give you the skill to brew it?' They all laughed.

'Whilst I've been in London I've become more than a millwright.' Henry looked surprised. 'I call myself an engineer now,' George continued, 'because it's a more general skill. Employers are looking for men to keep their machines going. And there are more and more of them. It seems as if everything will be done by machine soon. At this rate there'll even be machines making machines by the time our grandchildren are men!'

'Well I suppose our grandfathers would be amazed at seeing machines ploughing the fields without a horse to pull them!' interjected Freddie.

'But what about you and your family?' asked Henry. 'You're taking quite a risk, moving your family here without the certainty of regular work. I could ask Mary at the yard – she'd say yes if I said we needed you.'

'Come back to the yard with Edmund as the master?' George shook his head.

'But we never see him!' exclaimed Freddie.

'I heard about the will. What do you think will happen when Mary's gone? I know she's strong but she is old and she'll not live forever. No, I'd rather find something independent of Spandler's yard – and I know I'm skilled enough to do it.' Abruptly Henry kicked the gate and left.

'What?' George looked horrified.

'You've just talked about the very thing that frightens him.' Freddie frowned but George chuckled.

'I'd forgotten how funny that scar of yours is when you're trying to be serious.'

Freddie smiled but then shrugged his shoulders. 'I often wonder what will happen.' He looked at his brother. 'I've been thinking about looking for other work myself. I know Henry realises there's a problem because he's made sure his boys are apprenticed somewhere else.'

'Is that so? Why does he not leave then?'

'He promised Uncle Robert. He knows Aunt Mary would be upset if he left. But it's more than that – I fear he still holds onto a dream that one day the yard might be his.'

'Ed is not well. Perhaps if he pre-deceased his mother?'

'Perhaps, but it would have to be unexpected because Ed hates Henry,' explained Freddie. 'All the time his father was alive he would tell Ed how much better he thought Henry was than him – and then he put Henry in charge of the yard in his will. Ed would do all he could to stop Henry ending up with it. Probably already has.'

'I can remember Ma calling at the yard when I was small and Ed knocking me over with the broom. I suppose he'd been told to sweep up and I was in the way. I fell and bloodied my knee and he laughed.'

'Not a pleasant person, Edmund. He taunted me about my scars the first day I started work. He was always alone but it was his own fault because no-one wanted his company.' The conversation ended because Ruth called out that tea was ready. The two men went indoors.

Meanwhile Henry had turned left at the end of Vauxhall Gardens along the road towards Caister. He was walking very quickly, barely aware of his surroundings; his mind screamed inside him.

Die! Die! Die, Edmund Spandler, die! The yard's mine. In all but name I've been master there these last three years and more. And it's made money in spite of those new millwrights that have started up. Ed's had plenty enough money from it so he must know that. Oh die can't you? Just drop dead – then I'm sure Mary will leave the yard to me!

He stood still as his mind ran the alternative.

When Mary dies he'll come back as master, telling me what to do, challenging my decisions. I'll hate it and so will the men. I won't be able to get them to work like they do now because he will destroy them. He's already told his mother that he wouldn't employ a cripple so young Tony will be out.

He was hit by several large raindrops and looked up: dark clouds had gathered. He realised where he was and, with the likelihood of a soaking, he turned up the collar of his jacket and strode back towards Yarmouth.

The following month George's work on the monument finished but by then he had proved his worth at Lacon's. They took him on full time and at the end of the year they gave him a contract. Carrie returned home for the winter and found temporary work in the silk factory.

January brought snow. The road outside Francis buildings was hard and had formed ridges and grooves where carts had left their tracts and it had frozen. One evening at the end of the third week William burst into the house. 'Breydon water has iced over! People are skating on it!'

'Saturday tomorrow. Half day. Let's go then,' suggested Harry and Tom jumped up and down with excitement. One look at Henry convinced Eliza that she would be staying at home. She bit her lip.

Why shouldn't I go? Because I'm a girl and will show myself up I suppose – but I expect there'll be other girls skating. Why must I behave like a lady? Pa's been so sad since he came back that evening soaking wet. I would make him really cross if I asked him.

She sighed.

Will my life always be like this?

During the evening Mary-Ann looked from Henry to Eliza many times. Their expressions were the same, sombre and sad: father and daughter were alike.

16

It was the second of April 1861, the week after the census. Mary-Ann was keeping Henry's meal warm on a plate above a pan of simmering water. Earlier she'd served the rest of the family their meal because Harry and William had been in for a while and had been looking hungrily towards the kitchen. Now they had all long since finished eating and Henry still hadn't come in. Harry looked at his mother.

'Shall I see if I can find him?' Mary-Ann's frown deepened but before she could reply the door opened. Everyone stopped talking. Momentarily Mary-Ann smiled: Henry was sober; his face, however, had the appearance of stone.

'She's had some sort or fit. I found her on the floor in the cottage when I called in on my way out of the yard. Her face is all pulled to one side and she cannot walk. The doctor's with her now.' Henry spoke rapidly and tension overwhelmed them as they realised about whom he spoke. Mary-Ann shook her head even though the pallor of her husband's face agreed with his words. He sat down and put his head in his hands. 'I've been down to the Anchor to tell Edmund.' He looked at Mary-Ann. 'Would you believe he stared at me for a brief moment and then smiled? His own mother!' He shook his head.

Mary had had a stroke. It left her unable to speak or walk. Her mind was unaffected and she cried a lot. Robert Flowers's wife Elizabeth, who was her daughter, moved into the cottage to care for her.

Susan Flowers, Elizabeth's twelve-year-old daughter, was one of Eliza's friends. Eliza used to wait each morning until she knocked and then they would both call on Hannah and her younger sister Emily (Freddie's daughters) and the four girls would all walk to school together.

'This is my last day for a while,' said Susan the morning after her grandmother's stroke. Eliza closed the front door behind her.

'What? W-What do you mean?' stuttered Eliza.

'I mean I won't be coming to school. At least not for a while.'

'But why?'

'I'll tell you when Hannah's with us,' said Susan as they both turned up Vauxhall Terrace.

'Are you going to tell Hannah now and explain?' demanded Eliza as they turned back into Caister Road towards Northgate.

'My Ma started selling bread and pastries last year. She cooks them in her oven in our back yard. She uses Pa's flour and she has quite a few regular customers whom she doesn't want to disappoint. I help her when I'm not at school but now she has to go and look after grandma so I'm leaving school to do the baking.'

'Oh Sue,' wailed Eliza, 'poor you.'

'Actually I'm quite excited. I enjoy baking – and selling – and school is tedious. Last week we were learning how to make pastry! I was surprised at how many girls didn't know how but I think I could have taught the lesson. I'd be leaving next year anyway so I hope I won't have to go back.' Susan was two years older than Eliza and both she and Hannah were now in the senior department.

'I'll still be here when you move up next year,' said Hannah.

'I'm looking forward to it,' said Eliza. 'Miss Rauds came down to the juniors last week and her lesson was really interesting. I take my school test next month.'

'Yes, well, she does take the lower form,' explained Susan. 'But once you move from there it's all about how to be a woman when you get married. You'll pass the school test easily Eliza, you're so clever. But soon you'll want to leave as well.'

And then Pa will marry me to whoever it is he has chosen – perhaps not straight away. I'll be promised so that will be that. It all seems dreadful but I've just got to find a way of making it better for myself. Carrie's not let having James make her unhappy – and I even caught Pa smiling at him the other day. It's my life; I have to work it out.

Half way through the morning a senior school boy came to the classroom and handed a piece of paper to the teacher who looked around at the children: they were busy writing. Eliza was trying to work out what a word meant in her comprehension passage and had not noticed so she jumped when the teacher called her name. He told her that Mr Mounseer wanted to see her in his office. Her heart began to beat loudly in her ears because Mr Mounseer was the headmaster and pupils were usually only summoned to receive discipline: Eliza couldn't think what she might have done. A whisper went round the room as she put away her work. When she reached the office the door was open and Miss Rauds was there. She smiled but Eliza was not reassured.

'Is this the pupil?' Miss Rauds nodded. Mr Mounseer looked surprised. 'But she's a girl!' In spite of her fear Eliza struggled to remain silent.

Miss Rauds turned to her. 'Eliza, it is my job to look at all the work of the top classes from the junior department. I have found your work to be of an exceptional standard. I have recommended to Mr Mounseer that you do not take the school test but the grammar school entrance test instead.' Delight flashed across Eliza's face.

'I repeat, Miss Rauds, she is a girl.' Mr Mounseer was sounding impatient.

'The grammar school is taking girls for the first time this year, and –,'

'Miss Rauds you do not understand,' he interrupted, his face reddening with impatience. 'She is a girl. Even with the scholarship it would cost money and her family would need to agree. It would be a waste.' The words coming out of his mouth grated on Eliza like the sound that the teacher's chalk sometimes made on the blackboard. Reality crushed her.

Miss Rauds noticed. 'Eliza,' she said softly, putting her hand on Eliza's shoulder. Hesitantly Eliza lifted her hand and looked at Mr Mounseer. He nodded his permission for her to speak.

'P-Please S-Sir, I know you are right. But perhaps if you wrote to my fath...' Eliza's voice trailed off. In suggesting Mr Mouseer's actions she could be thought insolent. Her hands were clasped behind her and she dug her fingernails into her palm to distract herself from the impending tears.

'Eliza, return to class,' Mr Mounseer ordered. 'Miss Rauds and I will discuss this further.'

Later, walking home from school, she was euphoric: her schoolbag containing the letter felt light, almost explosive.

Henry read the letter and sighed. 'Why is it that my cleverest child is a girl?' He shook his head and looked at Eliza. 'The grammar school is the wrong sort of education for you.' Eliza looked past his shoulder to where a sunbeam had formed.

'You'll have a fine time in the senior department,' said Mary-Ann as gently as she could. 'Miss Rauds teaches the girls. Carrie enjoyed it.' Her voice went alternately loud and soft in Eliza's head. 'You'll learn how to make a man happy and look after his children well.'

As a good woman should. I knew that this is what would happen. This is as it's always been. I'm a girl and my education is unimportant. Why did I allow myself to hope?

Eliza's head drooped and her gaze moved to her father's shoes. Henry smiled to himself, confident of her eventual acquiescence. However, he had no concept of how worthless he made his youngest daughter feel and how much she despised him.

On Monday afternoon ten days later, Carrie, who had earlier returned to the Olivito's house to prepare it for the family, arrived back at Francis Buildings. A message had come from Mr Olivito to say that they were not returning to England. On her way home she'd enquired at the silk factory and they'd agreed to take her on. The following week they suggested she trained as a thrower and learn to use the machine that combined the silk that had been unwound from the cocoons. She was happier than she'd been since she'd left Palmer's. Eliza noticed.

Mary, Robert's widow, never recovered from her stroke. During the summer she weakened and eventually, in October, she died. On Saturday afternoons when she was alive Henry used to take the books up to the cottage, share with her what they had been doing, and show her the balances. Now Edmund came and looked at the books in detail especially the expenditure, interrogating Henry on why the money had been spent. Henry would find it irritating but the rest of the week Edmund left them alone. Henry shared with Mary-Ann one evening that it wasn't as bad as he'd thought it was going to be.

The year turned and one morning in January Edmund called unexpectedly at the yard. Some of the men had just returned from repairing a sluice pump on one of the marshes. They started work at eight. Henry usually called a break at eleven and this particular morning, it being very cold, he had brewed tea. Edmund arrived to find the men grouped round Bessie, warming themselves, as Henry emerged from the office with the tea.

'Henry, have you turned servant to wait upon our men?' Edmund laughed but then turned to the men and barked, 'Bessie's not there for you to warm yourselves but to power the tools. And you're paid to work with them!' The men looked at Henry who was ignoring Edmund and continuing to walk towards them with the tea.'

'Henry!'

Slowly Henry put down the tray he'd been carrying on a bench near the men. He looked at them and nodded towards the tea before turning to Edmund.

'The men break now for fifteen minutes and then work better, with fewer mistakes. Your father and mother both thought it was a good idea.'

'They are dead. I make the decisions round here now, cousin.' The men started to pick up tankards of tea. 'Back to work I tell you! I'll fire you!' Edmund shouted; he was pale and his lips were darkening as he spoke.

'If you fire them you won't have a working yard at all. I can't do it all myself and I can't see you doing much,' retorted Henry. A short laugh erupted amongst the men.

Edmund shrugged. 'Well, perhaps I'll just sell it all,' he said and walked quickly to the yard door. He rested with his hand on the door for a few minutes until he could breathe properly and then left without even looking back.

The men turned to Henry but no-one spoke.

'He'll not do that,' stated Henry. 'He's too fond of spending the profits.' The men nodded and drank their tea but some of them frowned.

The yard continued to be successful. People with whom Henry did business spoke with him as if he was the master, which he accepted. He was relieved that Mary's death had not resulted in the large changes he had feared. As the weeks went by he began to hope that this was how it would continue.

Then one Saturday Edmund closed the accounts book with a bang.

'Last night at the Anchor someone said I wasn't the master here,' he stated. Henry did not comment. The fat in

Edmund's double chin quivered as he turned his head to look into Henry's eyes. 'I put him right of course.' Henry held his gaze and his silence. Then Edmund sat back and waved his hands in the air. 'They can think what they like,' he declared, laughing, 'but we both know the truth.' Henry exhaled slowly. 'There's one other thing. The cottage is empty now so I'm moving back in. I..er..I,' he hesitated, 'I'm getting married tomorrow,' he finished with a rush, beaming uncharacteristically.

Henry smiled and his angst disappeared. 'That's wonderful news,' he replied, his enthusiasm genuine. 'Who is the lady? What a pity your mother didn't meet her!'

'We've been together for years and Ma wouldn't have liked it. That's one of the reasons I moved into the Anchor. Her name is Elizabeth Simnel, brother of Johnny who was with me at school. Their father was an auctioneer and my father and he had a disagreement over something at the auction, years ago.'

'I don't remember.' Henry shrugged. 'I had worries of my own at that time.'

'Well you couldn't even mention their name at home afterwards – but that generation has gone. It's us now. In fact, Elizabeth suggested I came to talk with you. Yes, I'm master here. It's my yard. However my father was right, you do it better than I ever could – and, really, I don't want to. A few weeks ago when I came here shouting at the men to get back to work I had one of my funny turns when I got back home. Afterwards Elizabeth talked to me. Told me to leave you be. She's right. This is the last time I will look at the accounts. My parents trusted you and I see no good reason why I should not do the same.'

Henry smiled again. 'I will do as good a job for you as I did for them.' He paused. 'But what about...?'

'My health? Yes, and I am taking on a wife. When I die the yard can be yours if you can raise the mortgage but it will be sold. I must make provision for her. But until then you are in charge here in all but name.'

'Thank you. I will tell you about any big decisions in the same way as I did with your parents.'

Edmund stood and held out his hand. Henry grasped it and the two men looked at each other and nodded.

That night Henry did not call in at the King's Arms on the way home, which was unusual: his mind was in a whirl as he tried to work out how he could raise a mortgage.

It was nearly Easter and Mary-Ann hummed to herself as she sewed. She glanced at two-year-old James who was playing in the pen which Henry had rebuilt. He babbled at her and she smiled in return.

I'm happy. It's good at the moment – Henry's not drinking. He told me what Edmund said and I was surprised – I thought he would not let Henry have the yard at any price. I hope Henry finds the money. Carrie's happy at the factory but I worry about Eliza – I wonder if she still thinks about the grammar school, although she doesn't seem to be unhappy in the seniors. Harry reminds me of his father when I met him, tall and strong, although he's more carefree than Henry. William's settled down, thanks to young Mary-Ann. He told me he was worried about his father finding out but Henry didn't seem concerned when the letters started coming here – I suppose he thinks that they're just writing to each other and they won't meet again. Tom will finish school this year – which might cause an argument because I think he still wants to work at the nursery. Louisa – I wish I knew what had become of her.

She dismissed that last thought before it took hold and just at that moment the door opened with a bang and Tom and Eliza came in from school.

'Liza!' Immediately he saw her James shouted to be picked up.

'In a moment James. I must drink.' Eliza took a cup from the shelf and went through into the kitchen area where, on a stout shelf in the corner, was a large brass urn with a tap at the bottom. It had been Harry's final apprentice piece. Harry was a hard worker and often did more than was asked, staying late if a customer wanted something urgently, so Mr Smithson had allowed him to keep it. It delighted Mary-Ann because she no longer needed to filter all their drinking water. Tom looked over Eliza's shoulder as it gurgled its emptiness.

'None left for me then? Never mind, it's nicer straight from the standpipe.' He picked up the urn and a large bucket which was also used to fetch water.

'Thanks Tom,' said Ma as he walked towards the door, 'I was hoping you'd do that when you came in.' Tom smiled over his shoulder as he left to go down to the street where the standpipe was. Eliza finished her drink and went to pick up James.

'Take your school pinafore off first,' Ma warned her. Eliza stopped and turned away from James. She'd only ever been caned once, when she was late, and she took great care that it didn't happen again.

June was hot and sultry that year.

'Will you take my arm and we'll stroll down to the sea?' Henry asked Mary-Ann one Sunday afternoon. She reached for her bonnet and cape.

'Carrie and I will cut some bread and cheese so we can eat when you return,' suggested Eliza.

Carrie looked up from the book she was reading. 'If we prepare it for about six o'clock?' Mary-Ann nodded as she stepped through the door which Henry was holding open for her.

There were now streets running from Caister Road over the Denes to the sea but Henry chose to take Mary-Ann up to Northgate and through St Nicholas' churchyard because that was their usual route: they'd walked that way since the days when they were courting. By this time the drain had been covered over and, although its presence could still be smelt, it was much more pleasant to walk through the graveyard now. Mary-Ann squeezed Henry's arm when they reached the gate where their eyes had first met when they were young.

They arrived at the seafront and after walking up and down for a while they found a seat. They did not speak but watched the many who were promenading. Mary-Ann felt herself to be in a comfortable daydream. The crowds started to thin out and eventually Henry stood to his feet.

'I think we need to go home,' he said, looking at the darkening clouds. Mary-Ann stood up.

They started walking. Henry spoke again. 'Tom will be leaving school soon.' The sudden comment startled her but he continued, 'I would have liked him to follow his brothers into Smithson's. I met Mr Mounseer. He doesn't think Tom is lazy, just not very clever. I wonder if I should allow him to work with Mr Greensome in the nursery,' he paused, 'but it won't be an apprenticeship.'

Mary-Ann heard his uncertainty and squeezed his arm again. 'He's a hard-working boy. I'm sure he'll do well for himself.'

'Well enough to support a family in the future?'

'He'd probably have to work very long hours to earn a good wage although I would think he knows that.'

'I think I will question him to be sure. And then he can decide.'

It was the Friday of the following week and Eliza and Tom left for what was to be Tom's last day at school.

'You're happy that you're leaving, aren't you?' Eliza asked as they approached Vauxhall Terrace.

'Yes!' Tom grinned at her. 'No more books and outside all day.' Eliza shook her head as Tom continued. 'Yesterday afternoon Mr Mounseer was droning on and on about some other queen from a long time ago. It was hot in our classroom and I'm sure everyone was nearly asleep. I kept myself awake watching a meat fly buzzing around. After today I will never have to do that again.' Eliza couldn't understand her brother and was perplexed at her own position.

Two years ago Tom wanted to leave and work for Mr Greensome but Pa said no, that he had to stay at school and work hard to become an apprentice. Mr Mounseer tells Pa that Tom is not clever enough so Pa lets him do what he wants. Mr Mouseer told Pa that I was clever, clever enough to do well at the grammar school but did Pa change his mind? No. It's as if he thinks that being a girl and being clever means there's something wrong with me. But that can't be right. Why did God give me this brain if he intended that all I should be was a good wife and mother?

17

Twelve months later a letter came through the door that would change their lives. Everyone else had gone to work or school but Mary-Ann was in and was looking after James. She picked up the letter and studied it. It was addressed to William and, although it was not young Mary-Ann's hand because she was used to seeing those letters arrive, it bore the same postmark. She placed it on one of the shelves above the table and during the day she kept looking at it. All she could think of was that it was from Christmas and she dreaded that he might be telling William not to write any more.

William arrived home before Harry or Henry because the two new spades and a barrow that Mr Greensome had ordered from Smithson's were ready and he'd left work early to deliver them. Eliza was already home and was sitting at the table finishing schoolwork. Mary-Ann heard him and came in from the kitchen.

'This came for you today,' she said as she handed him the letter. His eyes lit up but then he frowned when he looked closer. Slowly he walked over to the bench and sat down. Mary-Ann held her breath as he opened it and read. Then his smile returned and she sighed. Just at that moment Henry and Harry came in.

'It's from Uncle Christmas.' William waved the letter in their direction. 'He says that Mary-Ann is becoming very fond of me and he wants me to come and visit.' He held up a money order. 'This is for my travel.'

'Well I need to write to him and warn him about you then,' declared Henry. 'It would be wrong for me to sit here and let you ask her to marry you. As her father he needs to know you're damaged.'

William stood up and looked directly at his father. 'I will write to him myself but I will tell her when I see her. I shall go to Mr Smithson tomorrow and ask when he can spare me. They know I was hurt.' He pointed to the scar on his face.

'Well if I was he I would send you away and forbid my daughter to marry you. Marriage is for having children. That's what the Bible says.'

William had not taken his eyes from Henry's face. In contrast to his father his voice was quiet and controlled. 'Pa, I will be honest with them and Mary-Ann can decide. Or her father if he insists. I won't go against him although it will be hard if he says no and she still wants me.' Henry nodded curtly and sat down in his chair.

'Make sure you do just that,' he said as he picked up the newspaper and started reading. Eliza, watching from where she was still sitting at the table, was proud of her brother.

July turned out to be an eventful month.

It was early on the morning of Friday the tenth. Henry had already left because he and the men from the yard were working on Ormesby Broad and it would take them most of two hours to get there. Tom had left even earlier than his father because, being July, they were very busy at the nursery and when the sun was up he was at work. Harry had just left for Smithson's but not before he had shaken William's hand and wished him well. Eliza and Mary-Ann were sitting at the table eating breakfast of cold marrowbone broth left over from the previous evening's meal. The liquid had thickened to a jelly and they spread it on slices of stale bread.

'This is tastier than it was last night,' Eliza observed.

Mary-Ann nodded. 'Yes, it is. It seems to happen when it stands – but then in an hour or two it will have stood too long and be bad.'

Just at that moment William came through the door from the stairs carrying his bag. He had worked every Saturday afternoon and several late evenings since he'd received Christmas's letter and he was beginning his journey to Yorkshire later that morning. He would return on Monday. Eliza was pleased that Henry had gone to work. Earlier that morning he had been unsmiling and abrupt and Eliza had hated the tension. Now William was calm as he sat down at the table next to them. They didn't speak but quickly finished eating.

'Give our regards to Alfred,' said Eliza as she opened the front door.

'Not just Alfred,' added Mary-Ann. 'everyone else as well. I think Mary-Ann will be very grown up.' At the mention of her name William smiled briefly but then looked down at his bag and fiddled with the clasp. When he looked up Eliza had gone.

As Eliza walked up Vauxhall Terrace she thought of him.

He's been happy whilst they've been writing to each other. He still hates me for some reason – he really hurt me when he kicked me – then it wasn't long after that that we had the party for old Aunt Hannah who died last year. That's when Mary-Ann came. Uncle Christmas seemed such a genial man that I wonder if he would forbid her if she wanted to be with William. But would she want to once she knows? Would I want to marry a man and have no children? I know William wrote back to Uncle Christmas but I don't think he's had another letter.

Her thoughts turned to her day at school.

I wonder if Miss Rauds will ask me to help with the younger ones again – what would Pa say if he knew? It was hard last time. I had fifteen children in my group and most were good but there were three boys who kept saying they didn't know how but I think they just didn't want to do it. I like learning and reading myself but I'm not so sure about becoming a pupil-teacher like Miss Rauds wants. I know how to do everything they teach girls in the seniors and Mr Mounseer won't let me listen to the boys' lessons. What will I do in school if I don't teach?

'Well it's done – I've asked her but I told her not to decide straight away. She'll write as soon as she has an answer.' It was Monday evening and William had returned.

'She knows everything?' Henry interrogated.

'Her father does – she knows there are problems. He and I had a long talk on Saturday afternoon and he took me to a doctor there.' William smiled. 'The doctor thought that it would be difficult but not impossible for me to father a child, which is better than I thought. He is going to send a written report to Uncle Christmas who has told me that he and Aunt Mary will explain everything to Mary-Ann. I will await the outcome.' Henry stood up and came over to his son, his hand outstretched.

'Well done son. This week you have become a man.'

'Yes,' William acknowledged with a smile, 'and I have made plans. If she cannot have me I will leave Yarmouth and make a new life for myself. Mr Smithson has family in Kent and I can finish my apprenticeship there. He was asking last week if anyone wanted to go. I know Oliver is going and we started at the yard together so I will go with him.' For a few moments everyone stood still as if frozen. Mary-Ann turned towards the kitchen, her lip quivering.

'Are you sure Will?' Tom asked.

'Why do you have to leave?' added Eliza. Mary-Ann had stopped by the door and Eliza reached up to her.

'Because this is where we met. I would be sad each time something here reminded me of her. This way I can forget.' He paused but then drew a deep breath and continued, 'and I have bad memories here as well.' He turned to Mary-Ann and Eliza. 'I'm sorry for those bad memories because we share them. That's another reason I'm going, so that you can live your lives without fear.' Eliza went to speak but William shook his head. 'No, I see the fear in your eyes sometimes. I know I wouldn't hurt you again but you cannot be sure. If she accepts me we will stay in Yarmouth but find our own lodgings somewhere. Whatever happens I will no longer live here.'

Eliza and Mary-Ann looked at each other and went into the kitchen. Eliza sighed and she realised that he was right: she did fear him and, although he was her brother and she loved him and would miss him, she was still glad that he would no longer live in the same house as her.

When Eliza and Mary-Ann returned from the kitchen with trays of tea William was talking with his father and brothers and his face was animated. 'They're coming I tell you. There was a lot of talk about it at the station. Have none of your customers come in with news of it?'

'Who's coming?' asked Eliza.

'The channel fleet. Don't you remember they came last year?'

'Seems strange that they visited before I was born and then they passed by on the open sea – until a few years ago,' commented Henry.' They came then and last year – and now they're here again.'

'But many people do well out of them.' Harry sipped his tea and smiled at his mother. 'Last year one of them lost an anchor and Smithson's made a new one.'

'Yes I remember,' said William. 'I wonder if Mr Smithson knows. There'll be visitors to the town and we could sell some trinkets to them.'

'We still have the moulds for those brass spoons we sold last year,' said Harry.

'I'm going to the yard.' William stood up. 'Mr Smithson's been good letting me have time off.'

'I'll come with you. You can't work on your own.' Harry had finished his apprenticeship that year and together they could be productive.

Harry and William left and Eliza went out into the kitchen to check that the water in the pan under Tom's meal had not boiled dry: he would be working until it went too dark to see.

18

The following day Eliza returned from school delighted with the news that it was closed for the rest of the week: so many children would take the time off anyway as soon as they heard about the fleet that Mr Mounseer had decided to set everyone the task of doing a written report about it and sending them home.

There was a knock at the door. Emily, Elizabeth and James were on the doorstep when Eliza answered it and Ruth, their mother, was standing behind them.

'Are you coming to see the warships come down the Roads?' asked Ruth from the doorstep. 'I thought we might knock at Jemima's house and see if they wanted to come.'

'We could call on the Flowers and see if Elizabeth and Susan are coming as well,' Mary-Ann called just before her head appeared around the door leading through to the kitchen; she grinned at Ruth.

'I thought of them but they're often busy,' replied Ruth as Mary-Ann and Eliza tied on their bonnets and laced up their shoes.

'Yes, I think they're probably up to their elbows in flour,' laughed Eliza. 'They'll not miss the opportunity to sell more.' She lifted James from the pen and sat him on the bench to put on his shoes. He beamed when he realised what was happening because he knew it meant that they were going out.

The house in Moat Street was similar to Francis buildings in that the front door opened directly into the living area. It was answered by Matilda, the eldest child of George and Jemima and the only survivor of their children born in London. She smiled when she saw Elizabeth, who, as well as being her cousin, was her best friend: they were the same age although Matilda was about a foot taller.

'We're going to watch the fleet,' Elizabeth told her. Jemima, at the back of the room, was cleaning the face of a small boy: this was Herbert the child she had been pregnant with when they had moved to Yarmouth. Matilda looked at her mother who nodded and they quickly scrambled into outdoor clothes.

As they walked down towards Blakes Buildings where Elizabeth and Susan Flowers ran a small bakery from their house, Eliza and Emily walked with two little boys, both called James between them and Herbert walked with Matilda and Elizabeth. Eliza missed Hannah who had just left school and was now working in the silk factory. Eliza was right about the Flowers: they quickly said hello but then sent them on their way. The group came down the side of Britannia Terrace onto Marine Drive near the pier: it was crowded with people who were looking towards Cockle Gateway, the passage by the north end of Scroby Sands, where the fleet was just beginning to enter into the Roads.

Scroby Sands were, and still are, sandbanks situated approximately a mile and a half from the Yarmouth shore. Between them and the steeply sloping shore there is a channel. The sands in this area constantly move and yet it is always deep enough to enable the anchoring of quite large ships where the sandbanks give some protection from the worst of the sea. This deep channel, known as Yarmouth Roads, can be viewed from Marine Drive and it was from there that they watched the fleet arrive. Eliza was sitting on the end of one of the seats next to Mary-Ann, Ruth and Jemima whilst Emily, Elizabeth and Matilda played with the boys on the sand. In a hundred and fifty years structures would be built upon Scroby Sands with arms which turned in the wind. Eliza and her family would have been puzzled: they would have recognised that they harnessed the power of the wind but, electricity being beyond their imagination, they would have wondered how people were expected to reach them with their grain, or even if they were trying to pump the sea away!

Eliza gazed at the children whilst the three women were talking together.

I can see my life before me. I will come and sit on one of these seats and watch my own children in a few years. I'll even get old here and see my grandchildren play on the sand. This will be all there is and yet I have to make myself happy in it. Carrie seems happy: she left for the factory this morning without any resentment that she would not see the fleet.

She watched James, James and Herbert laughing together as they dug in the sand.

Carrie's his mother; she should be able to see him having all this fun. She hardly sees him at all. It seems unjust.

'That's an enormous ship,' said Ruth as she watched the first of the warships come down the Roads. Her comment cut through Eliza's thoughts and she looked up from the children to the sea. It was indeed large, built on three levels with a row of cannon sticking out at each level. Eliza shuddered when she thought of how much damage that one boat could inflict if it started firing. That boat was followed by many others: they came into the Roads under steam power and anchored in two lines. During the process it was quiet: there were no shouts from the men in the boats, as you would have down on the Quay when merchant vessels jostled for position, because all their communication was done through the raising and lowering of flags on the flagship and each boat followed its orders in its turn. Even the huge crowd on the shore was quiet as they watched the choreograph: it was serene, almost elegant, and inspired admiration. When they were all at anchor the Volunteer Artillery in the town fired a welcoming salute. As the noise died away it was followed by a ripple of applause that swept the shore. By this time the women and children had been joined by Freddie, Henry and Harry. Tom was still at the nursery and William was filing and polishing the spoons to sell to the visitors who were expected to flood the town the following day. George, Jemima's husband, worked at Lacon's, the brewery and he was still at work. His engineering skills were fully employed keeping the machinery going whilst the brewery produced as much ale as it could: in the next few days all the beer houses in the town would sell as much as Lacon's could supply.

'If we want a drink we'll need to have one now,' said Freddie. 'Shortly the officers will start coming ashore and there won't be any for us!' He laughed and his one eye sparkled while the scar over his empty socket did a dance.

'Let's go to the old tavern,' suggested Harry. The old tavern was older than any of them knew and had served generations of fishermen long before the day-trippers had started to come. The men left. The ladies walked back into town and, at first, Eliza walked with her mother as she had on the way down. Carrie and Hannah had arrived from the silk factory and walked along with the younger children. Hannah looked round at her and beckoned her so she quickened her pace and joined them. As she moved away Ruth began to speak.

'I've enjoyed our afternoon together,' she said, 'it's a pity we can't do it again soon.'

'What about on Saturday,' Mary-Ann suggested, 'then Carrie and Hannah can come with us as well.'

'The men will want to see the ships,' Jemima pointed out. Mary-Ann found it hard to hear her because Jemima was tall yet quietly spoken.

Ruth pulled a face. 'I've enjoyed watching them today but I would rather do something else. Perhaps we could go to Beccles?'

'How would we get there?'

'What about the train? It would be quite an adventure,' suggested Jemima, her voice louder now, with excitement.

Mary-Ann looked doubtful. 'I don't think Henry would like it.'

'What do you mean?' Ruth asked with a frown. 'He doesn't need to miss the warships. We're a large group so we don't need a gentleman escort.'

'That's just it. He's very protective of us. He wouldn't be happy at the thought of us going on a train without him.'

Ruth snorted. 'Where would he think we were going? London? Now, on our own, that would be too exciting even for me.' Her eyes shone and Mary-Ann looked horrified. Five minutes later the three women caught up with their children who had come to a stop outside the house in Moat Street.

'Meet at the station – the one at Southtown of course – at one,' said Jemima as she went indoors. Eliza, Hannah and Carrie exchanged glances.

'We're going to Beccles on the train on Saturday afternoon,' Ruth explained. Carrie and Eliza looked hesitantly at Mary-Ann while Hannah, Emily, Elizabeth and Matilda jumped up and down and laughed together. The three boys, James, James and Herbert copied them although they did not know why.

Saturday morning arrived and Henry was still not happy: Mary-Ann had explained to him that the other families were going without their men and had tried to reassure him that they would be safe. He left to go to the yard at the same time as Harry and William left for Smithson's and earlier, before Carrie had gone to the factory, he had tried to ignore the excited female chatter in the kitchen as they decided what food to put in the basket to take with them. Eliza had been amazed at her mother who had refused to be denied the trip that the other women were having and had argued with Henry when he initially said no, pointing out that they went shopping on their own, including going to the fish-market where the men were rough and loud. Eliza listened to her father's continued opposition and realised his concern was about his control: never before had she known Mary-Ann do anything else but acquiesce and it heightened her excitement.

They met outside the station by the flowerbeds. Eliza thought the station looked very grand with two rows of large windows and an overhang that they could have sheltered under had it been raining. Hannah and Carrie were the last to arrive: they'd left the factory as soon as the hooter had gone and both of them were breathless having walked as fast as their dresses would allow. When they entered the station they were in a short corridor with a small window in the wall. Ruth stopped here and bought tickets for her family, then it was Jemima's turn. Eliza could see Mary-Ann becoming agitated. She looked at Carrie.

'Ma, if you'll give me the money for your tickets I'll buy them at the same time as mine,' Carrie suggested. 'Eliza can come to the window with me if she wants.' Eliza quickly stood with her sister at the window. In the room behind there were several men in smart uniforms.

'Second-class tickets for two women and a girl to Beccles and back, please. My little boy is three, do I need one for him?' The man shook his head as he leant towards a rack and took two tickets from one pile and one for another.

'The two full fares are one and six each and the half fare is ninepence so that's three shillings and ninepence altogether if you please ma'am.'

'Here you are Ma,' said Carrie as they left the window and she turned and gave her mother the tickets. At the end of the corridor they came into a large room that amazed Eliza. The ceiling was a full two storeys high and the room echoed when they spoke. It reminded Eliza of going into St Nicholas' church.

'Before we go out onto the platform we need to go into the ladies room,' said Ruth. The ladies room had rows of benches inside and as soon as they entered they could smell the privy.

'The children can go first,' said Matilda, leading the way through the door at the back.

'I won't be using it,' said Mary-Ann, 'and I would rather that Eliza didn't either.'

'Why not?' Ruth asked. 'Remember this is ladies only in here. Besides which, there is no privy on the train and the tracks, Freddie tells me, are sometimes very bumpy. Might be more unpleasant not to.' She chuckled and Eliza thought she was trying to make her mother more light-hearted.

'What harm can come of it Ma,' said Carrie. 'It doesn't smell too bad so they must be keeping it clean.' Mary-Ann did use it and when it was Eliza's turn she was fascinated to find that it wasn't just a seat with a bucket of earth beside it. There was a big wooden box behind the seat into which the words "earth closet" had been burnt and it had a handle. When she pressed the handle she could hear earth falling down into the hole. How clever!

They went through the doors out of the large room onto the platform. A train was standing there and its proximity made Eliza's heart beat louder.

'Is this the London train?' Ruth asked a guard. Mary-Ann looked shocked and Ruth laughed. 'It will be ours because the London train stops at Beccles,' she explained.

'That's correct Ma'am,' said the guard. 'It will be leaving in five minutes exactly.'

Quickly they all entered a carriage. Eliza, comparing it with stagecoaches that she had seen, thought it was enormous. It was divided into three small compartments and they entered the one on the right marked second class; the one in the middle said first class and there was another second class on the other end. The next carriage was third class and was nothing more than a goods wagon that had had the side walls reduced to half their size and a gate put in. The gate was swinging open and Eliza could see rows of wooden benches inside. As she mounted the steps into the second class compartment she saw two long wooden seats and another door and window at the other end. The seats backed onto the sides of the compartment and there was just enough room for all four adults including Carrie and seven children. As the last one entered the guard looked into the carriage.

'Destination please?'

'Beccles,' replied Ruth and the man promptly shut the door and locked the carriage.

'Does that mean we can't get out?' asked Matilda.

'Yes,' replied Ruth without concern. They'll unlock it at the other end.' They heard the guard blow his whistle.

'That means all the doors are shut. We're going now.' The children were in two groups at both the windows. Eliza felt her heart giggle as the train began to move.

'But it's going very slowly,' shouted one of the children.

'You wait and see,' said Jemima.

After a few minutes Emily said, 'The train is galloping now!' Everyone laughed. Eliza was exhilarated at the speed but she could see that her mother was no longer looking out of the window as the fields sped by. Then they began to slow down and came into a station.

'Belton and Burgh,' read Hannah. 'Isn't there a Roman fort or something like that here?' She instinctively turned to Eliza.

'Yes I was talking to some junior children about it only last week.' Mary-Ann looked up at her with a frown but looked down quickly: behind Eliza's head the scene outside was moving bewilderingly fast.

Eliza guessed that her mother was not enjoying her first train ride. Suddenly it went darker in the carriage as they entered Waveney Forest. Eliza was amazed to see how fast the branches were going by. After the next stop the train set off but did not pick up speed.

'Why is it not going fast?' asked Matilda, the disappointment showing in her voice.

'We're going to go over the river!' exclaimed Eliza who was sitting nearest to the window. The track had a slight curve in it as they left the forest which gave Eliza a view of the way ahead. The train was travelling slowly when they reached the bridge, so slowly that Eliza was sure she could walk as fast.

'Look Ma, look,' she said, 'it's beautiful.' Mary-Ann looked up and for the first time since they boarded the train she smiled. The sun was glinting off the water which disappeared in a straight line into the distance.

'I didn't realise the river was as straight as that!' she exclaimed.

'It isn't,' explained Eliza, 'it's been cut out of the marsh so that the bigger boats can miss out a loop in the river and reach Norwich. I read about it at school. Actually I think the river loops back on itself again before we reach Beccles so perhaps we'll cross the river again.'

'Look at all the boats,' called Emily from the other window. 'They're all looking at us!'

'That's because the train is crossing. When we've gone the bridge will swing out of the way and the boats can carry on down the river,' explained Eliza, pleased that the boys in her group at school had had lots of questions about trains so that she'd done lots of reading. She enjoyed telling other people things that she knew and they didn't.

After the bridge they came to Haddiscoe where the track crossed the line between Norwich and Lowestoft.

Here they passed over a set of points that made the carriage bump up and down. Mary-Ann looked alarmed.

'It's only the points,' explained Ruth. 'Think of them as ruts in a dry road.' Mary-Ann gave a weak smile. Eliza was fascinated by the number of tracks she could see. It appeared to her as if it was another world within her world. As they crossed the marshes Eliza noticed that her mother was now looking out of the window.

'It's Aldeby!' Ruth exclaimed. 'That's near Burgh St Peter where my parents live.'

'It takes ages in the gig,' added Hannah, 'we must come by train next time!'

'Yes I think we probably will. We only kept it on after moving from London to visit them. I think we could all come on the train for less half a crown. I don't know why we didn't think of it before, it's less expensive than hiring the horse.' She paused. 'However, Freddie does like his gig.'

They reached the second swing bridge which crossed the river next to a small wood and the train slowed down again.

'Look at the river winding off into the wood,' she said. Eliza thought it was pretty and all of them looked at it with wide-open eyes. They rarely came out into the countryside. Shortly after crossing the river they arrived at their destination and the guard unlocked their door. As she stepped off the train Eliza realised that if she had to walk it would take her a whole day to reach home. She had never been so far away. The thought exhilarated her.

From the station they walked through Beccles to the river. They passed the church.

'Look at the tower. It's separate from the church,' pointed out Jemima, 'how unusual. Perhaps we'll see if we can look inside after we've enjoyed our picnic.' After the picnic the adults wanted to sit and talk for a while and Hannah led the younger children in a game of hide and seek amongst the trees. Eliza looked at Mary-Ann who shook her head: she knew that Henry would ask that evening whether Eliza had acted like a young lady. Hannah raced past them shouting and Ruth laughed.

'Why don't you go and play with them Eliza?' she suggested.

'I can't, my father wouldn't like it.'

Ruth turned to Mary-Ann. 'I seem to remember you saying that when I suggested this trip.'

'I've defied him today by coming and bringing Eliza,' replied Mary-Ann. 'He'll want to know what she's done today.'

'So – then you don't tell him about hide and seek. Just tell him all about the train and the tower that we're going to see shortly.' Eliza looked at Mary-Ann who looked away. She looked at Ruth, grinned, jumped to her feet and ran off after Hannah. Ruth continued, 'Freddie would be upset if I lost one of them or if one of them was hurt. But playing hide and seek – he'd encourage them!'

'He only wants the best for her,' said Mary-Ann defensively.

'I thought we were going to look at this tower,' suggested Jemima. We want to leave ourselves enough time before the return train.'

Eliza found the tower fascinating and wished she could climb to the top. Ruth asked but was told it was too dangerous.

'Look at that,' said Matilda. She was pointing to a huge brown pot. 'The sign says it's a gotch.'

'It has something written on it,' said Ruth. 'Let's see if we can see what it says. She squinted at the writing which looked as if it had been etched into the wet clay when the pot was made. 'When I am filled,' she started.

'It would take a lot to fill that!'

'Six gallons the sign says,' read Eliza.

'When I am filled with liquor strong,' Jemima continued the verse. 'Each man drink once and then ding dong.'

Ruth laughed. 'That wouldn't suit your Henry!' Mary-Ann did not smile.

Jemima continued, 'Drink not too much to cloud your knobs, Least you forget to make the Bobbs.'

'His grandfather was a bell-ringer and would have known all about the Bobbs.' Mary-Ann's voice was quiet. 'Perhaps if Henry had kept on with bell-ringing he would never have turned to drinking so much ale.' Eliza was by her side in a moment.

'I'm sorry Mary-Ann. It must be very hard to live with.' Ruth had lost her smile.

'Ma it's a long time since he's come home drunk,' said Carrie. Mary-Ann nodded but she didn't reply. She knew that it was because he now hoped that the mill would soon be his. However she also knew that he had not raised the money and worried what would happen if he couldn't. She didn't think that his drinking days had ended.

On the return journey the train was full of holiday-makers.

'What are we going to do?' wailed Mary-Ann. Even Ruth was panicking because they could not see any empty second-class compartments.

The stationmaster was on the platform and saw their predicament.

'Is there not a carriage for you ladies? Well we cannot expect you to travel with them even if we could fit you in.' He jerked his thumb towards the third-class passengers. There seemed to be arms, legs and baggage everywhere; one woman had a large bundle on her knee whilst she balanced a young boy on the wall of the carriage with his legs hanging over the side. Eliza wondered why she did not put the child on her knee and balance the bundle. The stationmaster continued, 'A group of first class travellers have left the train. I think you should travel home in luxury.' With that he took their tickets and altered them.

In the compartment the seats had cushions and there were curtains at the windows.

'It's not as bumpy in here,' observed Mary-Ann as they crossed the points at Haddiscoe.

'That must be why the first-class compartment is in the middle of the carriage, so you don't feel the bumps as much,' suggested Eliza. 'The wheels were directly underneath us this morning.'

'Yes, you're probably right,' agreed Jemima. 'I didn't think of that.' Mary-Ann noticed that it was Eliza who had worked it out.

My clever daughter. What will become of her?

19

'Where's William?' asked Mary-Ann when they arrived home and only Henry and Harry were in.

'Gone to see Mr Smithson,' replied Henry. 'There was a letter from Mary-Ann for him on the mat when we got home. He went straight round to his house.'

'I know Mr Smithson's been asking him all this week whether he'd made up his mind or not. It seems he has,' added Harry.

The door opened and William entered. Everyone stared at him.

He laughed. 'It's me. I'm still here. I'm not a ghost.' He turned to Henry. 'Mr Smithson was pleased. Richard will travel to Kent a week on Monday and I may go with him then. He's written to his cousin. I'll know definitely next week.'

'So, Mary-Ann said no?' Eliza asked tentatively.

'She didn't say why.' William pushed his lips together. 'She did wish me well, though.' He smiled but it did not reach his eyes.

'And you're sure that you want to go away?' Mary-Ann's voice was steady. She looked into her son's eyes.

'Absolutely certain Ma,' he replied, without looking away.

Well that's it. I'm not going to teach any more.

Eliza was walking home on the Monday after the trip to Beccles.

I told Miss Rauds this afternoon. She said that if the boys would not do their work I could chastise them and she gave me a stick. But I enjoy reading and learning and I wouldn't want to have to beat someone to make them do it.

She says I need to talk to Pa because there's nothing else that they can teach me. I wonder what he will say?

Eliza decided to wait until after their meal had been eaten and cleared away. She would ask Henry when they all sat down but before Carrie started to read. They were reading a new book, 'The Mill on the Floss,' and she knew everyone would be impatient to get on with it. When she told him that she had been teaching the last few months he frowned which is what she had expected.

'I sent you to school for your own education, not to teach others,' he said. 'Why did you not tell me this was happening?'

'I was still learning things Pa,' she said, avoiding his question. 'I had to read up on each subject so that I could teach it and answer any questions they might have. However I do not like teaching because I am expected to force them to learn even if they do not want to. I was given a cane to use. I told Miss Rauds I don't want to teach and suggested that instead I used the books in school and learnt things by myself but she said Mr Mounseer would not agree to that.'

'But what about the things you're meant to be learning about, such as how to manage a home?'

'Miss Rauds said that I can do all of that and that going over it all again would be a waste of my time. I am with the senior girls sometimes – last week she was demonstrating suet pudding. She wanted to show how easy it was to double a recipe so I did a second suet pudding next to her with twice the ingredients. Er…she let me take it home and we all had it for dinner last week. Do you remember?'

Henry did not answer her question but instead turned to Mary-Ann.

'Did you know about this?'

'I..I..I knew about the suet pudding of course but I had no idea she was teaching all the time.'

Henry turned to Eliza. 'I will need to go and see Mr Mounseer. I am annoyed that this has happened and he has not let me know – I suppose it meant that he didn't have to employ another teacher. It cannot continue. If there is no longer anything there for you to learn it's time you finished with school.'

Henry's words entered Eliza's brain and ricocheted around her head producing a pain that felt as if they were trying to burst out of her forehead.

I thought he would tell Mr Mounseer that I must be allowed to use the school's books to teach myself. I didn't think he would tell me to finish school. Tom wanted to leave school early and he wouldn't let him, said that his education was important. But why am I thinking about Tom? This is me and I'm a girl. It doesn't matter if I learn because the only thing that's important is that I marry well. Why do I keep expecting it to be different?

Henry was speaking again.

'Carrie, are they looking for new workers at the factory?'

'Yes but Eliza's too young to do anything other than thread joining. Don't make her do that Pa. It's dangerous. A girl had her face cut open last week – she lost an eye.'

No one spoke. Eliza could hear the sound of her own breathing. The boys were standing in a group by the door and she wondered if they were about to go out.

'You can stay at home with Ma. She will finish your education. You may know a great deal about how to run a home but you do not know how to behave as a woman. You must not make decisions about what you do. You should have asked me as soon as they wanted you to teach at school. I direct your life, as your husband will in the future. This is the education that you need. This is what you must learn.' With that he strode over to the door and went out. The boys followed him. 'The Mill on the Floss' was forgotten.

The following morning Eliza went to school, returned some books and told them she was leaving. As she walked away her head still hurt: she'd not slept, having spent the last fifteen hours wrestling with her anger. She came back through the Shambles area of the market because Mary-Ann wanted her to pick up some cow shins. As she bartered with the butchers and returned their banter with interest her anger lessened.

Well I suppose this is better than having to sit through the seniors' lessons – but I'll miss the books though. I don't think that butcher wanted to sell me all these shins for ninepence. I saw him glance at the stall next door to see if they'd heard! While I was buying six I thought it only fair that he dropped the price. I wonder why Ma wants six?

'It's the town bazaar on Saturday,' Mary-Ann explained when she arrived home. 'I'm helping Mrs Rivers with her stall. Last year we made family dishes, which the ladies could buy to take home for an easy dinner, but no one would pay much. So this year we're making small things that people can eat there if they want.'

'You'll probably make more money that way,' agreed Eliza.

'It's for the town charities. Places like the Fishermen's hospital and the workhouse.' Eliza nodded and smiled.

I've decided to enjoy this. I'm not going to think of the future.

'So are we making meat pies with these – small ones that you can hold in your hand and eat? And perhaps we could also sell some soup from the cooking liquor. We'd have to think up a way of keeping it warm though.' Mary-Ann smiled as she watched Eliza talking enthusiastically.

During the week William came home with the news that he was going the following Monday. Mary-Ann fussed, wanting to make him new clothes to take with him, but he insisted that there was plenty of wear in what he already had and he didn't want to take too much with him on the journey. He was clearly excited at the thought of his new life: Eliza was pleased that he seemed so happy although she didn't understand her own feelings which were tinged with sadness.

Saturday morning arrived and Eliza and Mary-Ann were up early to bake the pies that they had made: they could only fit eight in the tiny oven and had to cook them in many batches. Henry had left Freddie in charge of the yard that morning in order to help them. He had made two large hay boxes in which to keep the pies and soup warm and he brought the cart down from the yard to transport them to the town hall.

Many people came to the bazaar with their own cup in the expectation that there would be refreshments on sale and for those that didn't they had a few that Eliza rinsed out in a bucket behind the stall. The pies sold well as did the bundles of cheese straws that Eliza had made out of the left-over pastry: small children bought them for a penny. During the afternoon a young man arrived and was introduced by Mrs Rivers as her son, Simon. Eliza judged him to be older than Tom but he was still talking about his schoolmaster. A couple of times Eliza tried to start a conversation with him and was disconcerted to find that he reddened and mumbled so she didn't try any more. She noticed her mother look at them whenever she spoke with him.

Is this the young man that Pa wants me to marry? She shuddered. *That makes it seem very real, as if it was going to happen tomorrow.* Her mind screamed and she turned to counting the money they had taken; she did her best to dismiss the thought.

Monday morning arrived. Henry, Harry and Tom shook hands with William before they left for work.

'Ma,' said William after they had gone, 'will you come down to quay to see me off this morning. Richard's family is coming.' He turned to Eliza. 'You can come as well if you want.'

'Yes I'd like that. I'm pleased we're parting as friends. I didn't like it when you didn't like me.'

'I don't understand it really,' said William. 'For some reason I have always blamed you because I was hurt, but I don't know why.'

'But,' Mary-Ann looked between her two children; 'don't either of you remember?'

'Remember what Ma?' asked Eliza. Mary-Ann drew a deep breath. 'Let us sit down together. I will tell you what happened.'

They sat together on one of the benches, Mary-Ann between her two children, whilst she recounted the story of that day when Eliza was three and William had tried to defend her. She told them how badly hurt he was and how Eliza was upset and tried to help care for him. Then she described how, from when he first regained consciousness, he seemed to hate her. She confessed that no-one had known what to do.

Eliza and William reached across their mother to each other. Mary-Ann quickly stood up and climbed out from between them, pulling them together as she did so. She stayed like that for some five minutes, with her arms around them, while all of them cried.

For the next few hours Eliza delighted in her brother but it was a poignant happiness. Now that she had him back he was going.

When Eliza turned from the quay you would have expected her heart to be light. She had been reconciled to her brother who'd been the greatest fear of her childhood; he had just sailed away and she was free of that fear.

William has gone. He's gone to make his life, in charge of his own destiny. Oh I wish I was him! Others decide my destiny and I am expected to be happy with that. I wonder if Pa will allow me to go and work in the factory when I am older or whether I will just stay at home with Ma learning to be submissive until he makes a good marriage for me? I will be a woman and will therefore have a woman's restrictions. That will be my life. But I will find my own way.

Printed in Great Britain
by Amazon